W9-ASI-675

DEC 1981
RECEIVED
OHIO DOMINICAN
COLLEGE LIBRARY
COLUMBUS, OHIO
43219

"Off to get my head together. I'll be in touch."

And with that note Dad is off for Denmark in the company of an adoring student, leaving behind a bouncing check at the local travel agency and a devastated wife Althea and daughter Jen to make the best of things at home.

Jen—always the witty and knowing observer and in many ways a mother to her own mother—stands by as Althea searches for fulfilling relationships and purposeful involvement. The quest carries her from one disastrous liaison to the next: from Percy (El Cheapo) to Sam (he'd make a good grandfather); from serving humanity which produces Freddy (ex-con but not fully reformed) to Henrik (a good guy); from Florida to the Catskills, and finally to a woman's group where Althea finds herself at last—and just in time, too, because Jen has met Peter (a prince) and is ready to give up mothering and be a teenager herself for a change.

Sheila Schwartz has caught all the funny moments of a family crisis in her first novel—a tender, heartwarming story about adolescence, a mother's and a daughter's, and growing up together.

(Like Mother, Like Me)

JF Schwartz
Schwartz, Sheila, 1929-
Like Mother, like me : a
  novel

LIKE MOTHER LIKE ME

a novel by

Sheila Schwartz

Pantheon Books

J
S

Copyright © 1978 by Sheila Schwartz
All rights reserved under International
and Pan-American Copyright Conventions.
Published in the United States by Pantheon
Books, a division of Random House, Inc.,
New York, and simultaneously in Canada by
Random House of Canada Limited, Toronto.
Manufactured in the United States of America.

10   9   8   7   6   5   4   3   2   1

Library of Congress Cataloging in
Publication Data

Schwartz, Sheila.
Like mother, like me.
Summary: When her father abandons his
family for one of his students, a sixteen-year-
old girl witnesses her mother's painful but
often comical metamorphosis into an
independent person.
[1. Mothers and daughters—Fiction]
I. Title. PZ7.S4113Me [Fic[77-26695
ISBN 0-394-83755-X

To my children,
Nancy,
Jonathan,
and
Elizabeth

114954

(Like Mother, Like Me)

(*one*)

My father

was an English professor at a small college in up-state New York. Last year, shortly before my fifteenth birthday, he skipped off to Denmark with one of his adoring undergraduate students. He didn't say good-bye to either my mother or me, just left a note: "Off to get my head together. I'll be in touch." That note tells you a lot about my father: He wanted to be a kid again. I want to tell you about the year he was away, and how my mother turned into a teen-ager and then grew up.

Both of my parents taught at the same college, so

my mother and I were able to manage financially when my father took his leave without pay. I don't know how he managed—maybe his eighteen-year-old had some money. I do know, for certain, that he had nothing.

All the years of my growing up I listened to my parents argue. The thing they fought about most was money. My mother would moan that their university degrees were only certificates that gave them the right to starve for the rest of their lives. Daily she would regret, and loudly, the fact that she had married another teacher.

Of course, you had only to look at my father to see *why* my mother had married him. My father could compete for the title of Handsomest Man in the World. A tall, ruddy, blue-eyed, tawny-haired Viking astride a ship bound for the New World; proud, fearless, straight, and super cool. That describes my father. In fact, he was so gorgeous that it took people a long time to figure out that he wasn't very bright. As soon as he would walk into a room, men would stand taller and women would swoon. Everybody was taken in by that impressive exterior.

At times it really seemed as if all he had to do was *be,* and people would eternally twinkle up at him. But he wasn't only handsome; he was nice. I think there's a great deal to be said about the good effects of good looks on the disposition. When everybody admires you all the time, you get accustomed to an accepting, non-hostile world. And this makes you very sweet. It also tends to make you weak and lazy, and non-competitive, since everything has always come your way so easily.

The fact that my father wasn't too bright was not apparent during the early part of his life. He came from a small midwestern town where nobody went to college. Dartmouth was glad to find somebody from his area; he provided a regional "balance." At Dartmouth, my father looked so handsome on skies that nobody really noticed his lack of mental ability. Oh, some professors may have suspected it, but they felt so guilty in the face of my father's unvarying niceness that they repressed their suspicions.

My father was elected to Phi Beta Kappa because, in addition to being nice, he was very good at memorizing. Then he got a fellowship to do graduate work, completed it, and received his M.A. But that was as far as he could go. He never completed his doctorate because he was never able to write a decent article. He misspelled, hated reading, got lost in poetry, and didn't like teaching.

But he was loved. My father was loved so much

that the English department voted unanimously to give him tenure even without his doctorate. They once loved him enough to give him the chairmanship of the department, but he loused everything up and they quietly took it away again. By the time of his defection, all they would let him teach was Freshman Composition—a real disgrace, according to my mother. But my father didn't care. He didn't care about a lot of things that seemed to matter to most people.

His students also loved him. They were always swarming about him—in his office, at the house, or telephoning him on one pretext or another. My mother's attitude toward students was very different. She regarded her home as a sanctuary from the students. I think she also felt that it would somehow not be appropriate for young men to drape themselves about her the way my father's women students did about him. "I should show them the picture in the attic, Dorian Grey," my mother used to snarl at him. He'd laugh, mildly.

His students loved him for the same reasons that I loved him. (Notice how I put that in the past tense. I still like him, moderately, but that is as strong as I would care to put it.) My father's students loved him because he was never in a hurry. He'd sit and share a pitcher of beer with them at our local pub and make them feel as good as if they were students at Harvard. He'd make them feel special. He was nice, kind, a good listener, and so pleasing to look at. He didn't have a mean bone in his body and was probably the easiest grader at the college.

Even before his defection, I had gradually come to realize that my father was a fine fellow to split a pitcher of beer with, but not someone you could depend on for anything. He seemed to have no memory. Here's an example of what I mean.

My mother would ask my father to pick up something at the store, say, a dozen eggs and a container of skimmed milk. Since we had only one car, and live four miles from town, there was no way for her to get the items once he had gone. Then she'd wait. And he wouldn't return. Four hours later he would come home without the items, having been sidetracked by a few of his worshiping students. My mother would start to foam at the mouth and my father would look at her uncomprehendingly.

"Why are you so upset?" he would ask. "It's only a dozen eggs and a container of milk. I'll go downtown and get them now. Why do you make such a big deal out of everything?" He honestly couldn't understand that she had waited all day for these things. He also couldn't understand that she might have been worried about him. He would never knowingly have upset her. That was just the way he was.

He had other unlovable qualities. He was always late. He was often absent. He would get caught up in projects that never got finished: a woven canoe, a solar greenhouse, yoga, homemade wine, a vegetable garden which produced the ugliest zucchini I've ever seen, repapering the kitchen, putting down a brick walk. The wreckage of his uncompleted projects was always around us, causing us to live in a limbo of nonaccomplishment.

His financial habits were interesting, too; his checks were always bouncing. He never remembered to carry money (lots of time he didn't have any), and so, if he ran into his claque, he would have to write a check. It never occurred to him not to foot the bill. He carried one or two loose checks in his pocket but never bothered to enter them in the checkbook or to see if there was any money in the account. My mother would seethe with embarrassment and go down to make the bad check good. The people at the bank liked him, so they were patient.

"If at least he drank," I'd hear her moan on the phone to *her* mother in New York City, "then there would be a reason for his behavior." My mother was big on "reasons" for things. She believed that if you could just find out *why,* everything would fall into place. "People really want to be rational" was one of her favorite educational theories.

I guess you can see by now that my father's handsome face had long since ceased to charm my mother. So when he defected to Europe, leaving a bouncing check at the local travel agency, she vowed she would never again love a handsome man. "The world lets them remain infants," she said.

"It's ridiculous to think that all handsome men are no good," my grandmother said.

But my mother was adamant. And one month after my father's departure she found a man who would have lost a beauty contest to Toulouse Lautrec.

Ugly Percy was as far as anyone could get from my father. He had "things" all over his face—I think they're called *wens*—the kind that could easily have been removed if he had not been too conceited to find any part of himself unattractive.

In fact, an interesting thing about this creep was

that he was a lot more vain than my father. My father would spend one minute in front of the mirror. He knew how he looked from the admiring stares of other people. But Percy was always looking at himself, smoothing down his remaining hair and making faces in the mirror in a futile attempt to look like male models on TV.

Percy had a round, bald spot in the middle of his head, like a medieval monk, and he combed his hair sideways to try to cover it. And the large pores on his nose made it look like the rutted surface of the moon. As if that weren't enough, he had a wispy little Fu Manchu goatee.

His flabby little body went with this face. Maybe because my father and I are tall, small men look unattractive to me, but this one had tiny hands and feet and there was no size or breadth to him. He was too petite, too lightweight, too unfinished-looking. Petite looked O.K. on my mother, but it looked peculiar on Percy. I didn't know anything about his ex-wife, but I had to believe that she and my mother were the only women who had ever found him attractive.

And to cap everything else about him, he was even poorer than my father because he was paying alimony and child support. But my mother didn't care.

In addition to the marvelous fact that Percy was ugly, he had his doctorate and was a full professor at Columbia, a first-rate university.

"Just imagine," my mother would drool, "a full professor." I grew up hearing about full professors. That's the top of the academic ladder. When I was little, I used to think that if you weren't a *full,* you were a *half,* or a *quarter,* or a *third.* Instead, the ranks go like this: lecturer, assistant, associate, and finally—the trumpets sound—a full. My mother was an associate, my father had been an assistant. But noble Percy was a full.

My mother was also impressed with his so-called erudition. Percy was a Laurence Sterne nut. Sterne wrote a book called *Tristram Shandy,* in the eighteenth century. He was also a clergyman. Well, Percy spent most of his spare time raising funds for the preservation of Sterne's ancient home in England. Everyone seemed to almost collapse at Percy's selflessness in constantly dragging himself over to England in an attempt to combat the indifference of the British to their own heritage. I didn't think he was so noble. My feeling was "Yankee, go home." Since nobody had asked him to do this, I didn't have much sympathy for his self-sacrifice.

Besides, if he worked all week and was with us

every weekend, I wondered when he saw his ex-kids by his ex-marriage. I was even more unsympathetic to his selflessness because, when I asked my mother how come she fed him every weekend and he con-tributed nothing, she told me that all his spare cash went into the Laurence Sterne Fund. I think it's kind of stupid to spend all your money on a dead man's house in England, while you eat and drink a family like mine further along the road to ruin.

One of the things that absolutely killed me was the way my mother waited on the little creep. Every weekend Percy was wined and dined at our house like a king (this description is my grandmother's). As I mentioned, he contributed not one penny toward food. In fact, if my mother failed to provide the Freihofer chocolate chip cookies he could devour by the box, he would complain. Only once, in a show of bravery, did she send him downtown to get his own box. And he did. But he brought it back, ate some of the cookies, drank up all the milk in the house, then put the unfinished box of cookies in his suitcase to take away with him.

Another time he brought a box of chocolate doughnuts with him. They were on the kitchen table. I ate one. "Who took one of my doughnuts?"

he stormed while finishing off the last of our diet soda. Do you think my mother said one word? She didn't. I almost burst.

Percy would bring his laundry to our house on Fridays, and my mother would do it for him before he returned to the city. Once she asked me to do it, and I refused. Percy shook his head sadly and said, "I can't stand the way she exploits you, Althea."

Me exploit her? My God, the pot calling the kettle. I didn't even know what the word meant at that time. But after I looked it up I knew that I now had found exactly the word to describe him. Percy never did anything for her. They never went out to dinner. Not once. Every weekend, three meals a day, she would wait on that little creep. She had never waited on my father. "I'm not your maid," she used to scold my father. So why was she so nice to this awful stranger? If my father asked her to do anything for him she would get furious and launch into a tirade how when both people worked they should divide the work up fifty-fifty and nobody should wait on the other person, and on and on. She was absolutely right, of course. So why was she waiting on Percy?

She was certainly Percy's maid. Percy liked Chinese food, so she bought a wok. Percy liked very dry rice, so she bought a steamer. Percy had a passion for straw mushrooms, so she rushed off to the gourmet shop and bought them at $1.29 a can. Percy would eat only brown rice from the health food store so she would make a special trip to get some.

I was revolted by her subservience to him. She would put a meal in front of him and humbly stand there waiting for him to taste it and give his approval —like El Exigente, the coffee authority, who sends whole villages into paroxysms of delight when he likes their local bean.

"Why does she do it?" I asked my grandmother. My grandmother didn't answer me, but she gave my grandfather one of those significant looks. I still didn't understand.

About a month after Percy's first visit, my mother told me nervously that he was going to sleep over that night. That sounded reasonable to me. They were going to a late party and we live seventy miles from New York City.

"I'll be quiet in the morning," I said, thinking that this was what was making her nervous.

I woke up in the middle of the night and went for a glass of water, passing the room in which Percy was supposed to be sleeping. The door was open, the bed untouched. I was ecstatic at the thought that he had gone home and my mother and I would be alone on Sunday.

But the next morning, there was Percy in the kitchen, wolfing down hunks of Jarlsberg cheese and gallons of orange juice. How could such a tiny man eat so much? He probably stoked up over the weekend at my mother's expense and ate corn flakes for the rest of the week.

After that, Percy was ensconced in her room every weekend.

I tried to talk to her about his sponging. "Mom," I asked, "doesn't it bother you that Percy empties out our refrigerator every weekend and never replaces anything?"

She was embarrassed. Finally she said, "Yes, it does bother me."

"Did you ever try speaking to him about it?"

"Yes, I did."

"What did he say?"

"He was indignant. He said, 'Do I ask you to chip in for the gas it takes to get to your house? And last week I had a new muffler put on my car and it cost eighty-five dollars. Did I ask you to chip in for that?' "

"Mom, that sounds logical but it really isn't."

"I know," she muttered.

"So what are you going to do about it?"

"Nothing."

"Nothing?" I shrieked.

"I don't want to lose him," she mumbled.

"I'll say something."

"Don't you dare."

"But, Mom, he's eating up my future college tuition."

"Don't get melodramatic, Jen. I'll confront it again when I can."

But I knew she wouldn't.

I didn't like seeing a stranger in my father's bed. I never thought about sex when my father was home. Most kids don't. Maybe at the back of their minds they think their parents do it occasionally, but most kids prefer to believe that their parents stopped doing it years ago.

I think my parents really did stop. Perhaps that's why my father ran off with one of his students. The reason I think they had stopped was that I could walk into their bedroom at any time; the door was never locked. When I did walk in, they were never in bed. They regarded bed as a place to escape from.

(*one*)

I spent a lot of time in their room because the big color TV was there. Since both my parents were contemptuous of anything that wasn't on educational TV, I could watch whenever I wanted to. I loved to lie on the queen-sized bed with my books spread around me, watching TV.

But with Percy in my mother's room, it was goodbye to weekend TV for me. *They* did *not* leave the door unlocked. I must admit I was bothered by the sexual aspect of their relationship.

I suppose Percy's making a specialty out of Laurence Sterne paid off in one way because he was always being invited to lecture at conferences. But the people who ran the conferences never seemed to have any money, so Percy was always "donating his services." In addition, he informed us, "It is an honor to be asked." My mother always nodded enthusiastically when he said that. She thought he was very noble to donate his services.

He never donated them to us. When he reached us, he was too fatigued even to take out the garbage. He was exhausted from the terrible responsibility of making people understand the necessity to revere and preserve, etc., etc., etc. He was so tired that he had to spend a lot of his time in bed. When he wasn't dozing, he took showers. He took about four showers a day, leaving the bathroom absolutely soaking, and leaving us with a basket of towels to wash after his departure.

One weekend, he told us he was having trouble with hostile students who preferred Allen Ginsberg's work to that of Laurence Sterne. Apparently they preferred just about any contemporary writer to Sterne. I didn't blame them. I picked up a copy of *Tristram Shandy* and thought it was a rambling bore. Percy used to talk about how funny it was, but I didn't think it was amusing at all.

"Pearls before swine," Percy fumed.

Here, as in most things, Percy was completely different from my father. My father knew little, but everybody loved him. Percy was supposed to be a hotshot in the Modern Language Association, and students who listened to him could supposedly learn something they didn't know, but nobody liked him well enough to listen. Except my mother. And honestly, he looked down on her. She once told me that people who taught English had to look down on teachers of every other discipline. This was their only way to maintain some kind of self-belief.

My father walked through life like an amiable, affable, innocent child, kind of like Brutus in *Julius Caesar,* but Percy was like Cassius, mean, envious, paranoid. He would tell my mother about his myriad enemies, and instead of telling him to knock it off and go for a walk, she would agree with him that the world is envious of geniuses, of the "bringers of truth," as they put it. My father would have squashed Percy like a cockroach, or laughed at his pretenses. My mother and Percy didn't have one sense of humor between them.

We had just read *A Midsummer-Night's Dream* in school, and I could see that my mother was like Titania, bewitched by an ass. I assumed that eventually she would recover from her bewitchment, but by that time I would have missed an awful lot of weekend TV.

But because I loved my mother and understood that it had really been a shock to her when my father left, I stopped saying anything critical of Percy after a while. "You wouldn't like me to criticize your friends," she said one day. I had to admit that what she was saying made sense.

Of course, I really didn't have any friends for her to criticize. I got along all right with the kids in school, but nobody lived near me. After I took the bus home from school, I was kind of isolated. I didn't mind too much because there wasn't much time. I did my homework, watched TV, helped Mom a little with the housework, and then it was time for bed.

I didn't have a close girl friend, and I didn't have a boy friend either. No boy had ever asked me even to go to the movies with him, although sometimes I went with a whole crowd of kids. Maybe my psychology teacher in school was right. He said we unconsciously telegraph our wishes to people. The truth was, I didn't feel ready for dating or going steady, and I was glad nobody had asked me. Anyway, most of the boys my age were covered with zits. Also, it seemed to me that I would need some time to recover from what had happened between my mother and father.

One more thing I want to tell you about my mother. She had been a high school English teacher when she met my father, and she had fallen as madly in love with him as his students later did. She could have no more children after me, so while I was growing up she had earned her doctorate in education. She had done it so easily that it was hard for her to understand my father's difficulties. But she was determined and able to concentrate. To his credit, my father never felt the slightest bit threatened by this. I used to hear him bragging to people about how smart my mother was.

She had obtained a teaching position in the Education Division of the same college as my father. In her heart, though, she remained an English teacher in high school, and perhaps that is why she was so impressed with Percy. Or maybe she was impressed by the fact that he taught at Columbia, while she would probably never get a better job than her present one at the state college. She was an academic snob, and she learned to be even more snobbish through Percy. As I said before, she didn't just love him for being ugly. She loved him because he had his doctorate; he did not have my father's inability to complete anything.

At Christmastime, the MLA (Modern Language Association), their big-deal organization, held its annual meeting in New York City. My mother went with Percy. "Everybody knew him," she proudly reported to me. I wanted to say, "Yeah, but did anyone like him?" but restrained myself.

Percy's attitude toward me was infuriating. One

night we charcoal-broiled dinner. My mother had paid for everything, as usual, and I had made the fire and watched the chicken. When we were eating, we found that one piece of chicken was underdone. My mother asked Percy to put it back on the fire—he had done nothing up to that point but eat—and he objected.

"If Jen were my daughter," he intoned, *"she'd* take the chicken back out. *She* undercooked it."

"I wouldn't have you as my father," I blazed back.

"Thank heavens," he said with that dumb pompous look on his face.

Trouble was brewing; it was inescapable. These are the events that led up to the fight.

My mother had won the first raffle of her life, in our local supermarket. It was a week's vacation for two in Florida, all expenses paid. I had never been to Florida and looked forward to sand and beaches, especially since we lived in the mountains. We had read a Ray Bradbury story in school, "All Summer in a Day," about a girl called Margot who goes to live in Venus, where it rains all the time. She hungers for the sun. That was the way I felt about a beach. I daydreamed about finding shells, walking with my mother, feeling tropical air on my face.

Now, to be fair, my mother never exactly said she was taking me, but then it never occurred to me that she wouldn't. I hadn't been anywhere but to my grandparents for about six years. I began to suspect something when I asked her when we were going to get me some resort clothes and she didn't answer. I figured maybe she was short of money and that we'd go shopping the last Saturday before the trip, which was to coincide with our spring vacation. So on that final Saturday, at breakfast, I asked if we could get the clothes that day. I was feeling a little anxious about it.

For once, King Percy had roused himself and was sitting at the breakfast table with us, devouring everything in sight. Percy, who prided himself on his directness, looked at me and said, "You are not going to Florida. You will be spending your vacation with your grandparents. Your mother and I will be going to Florida."

I wanted to cry. I couldn't believe my mother would do such a thing. "Is that true?" I asked.

She couldn't face my eyes and looked down at her plate.

I was suddenly filled with rage. I picked up the frying pan and went after Percy. That cowardly weasel, over whom I towered, frantically pushed his chair back from the table, let out a high-pitched wail, tripped on the hem of his seedy bathrobe, and fell to the floor. I landed on him full force, rearing back to hit him with the frying pan.

"She's going to kill me, she's going to kill me!" he screamed. "What will happen to my work. Protect me."

"Stop this nonsense, Jen!" my mother said, taking the frying pan out of my hand. Then she grabbed my wrist and pulled me off Percy.

"It's him or me." I started to sob. "It's him or me!"

The weasel, standing up to all of his five feet three inches now, shrieked, "She's mad, she's mad. Probably on drugs. This is what comes of your permissive tactics, Althea."

"You're the one who's mad," I screamed. "And you're even crazier," I screamed at my mother. "How can you sleep with this pukey little thing? He makes me want to throw up. His hands are too small and his head is too small and his brain is the size of a walnut. His dumb research is pukey. Who cares about Laurence Sterne?"

"Will you please go to your room?" my mother said.

I continued to scream at him. "You're a sponger,

a taker, a cheapskate. My mother's crazy to put up with you and everybody knows it. You big fake! How come you never even bring a bottle of wine? Cheapskate! Cheapskate! Cheapskate!"

"Oh, Althea," he moaned, "is this what you say behind my back? I'm crushed. How could you be so petty? I took you to the MLA. I introduced you to my friends. I was going to introduce you to the governing board of the Laurence Sterne Society. And all the time, behind my back, you were begrudging me the food and bed I thought we shared in such happiness." He was holding his forehead in his hand like Rodin's *The Thinker,* shaking his head tragically, reveling in self-righteousness.

"She didn't say a word, El Cheapo," I snarled. "I'm the one who sees you eating up my college tuition. Why should we pay for all your food?"

He turned a sorrowful gaze on my mother. "Do I ask you to share my expenses of driving up here?" he asked. "Did I ask you to chip in for my new muffler?"

"Stay home, El Cheapo," I said, "then nobody will have to pay for anything."

I dashed to my room and turned on my stereo full blast. I felt pretty good. What a joy finally to tell that creep off. Unfortunately, I didn't think it would make him stop coming. After all, where else could he find a totally free weekend retreat. Chip in for the gas! The nerve of that little turd.

My mother knocked on my door, and I decided I might as well face her. I unlocked the door, and she came over and sat down on the edge of the bed. I lay down on it and looked up at her. "Did El Cheapo leave?" I asked, hopefully.

"Why don't you stop this ridiculous act?" she said. "He actually thought you were going to hit him with the frying pan."

"I wouldn't touch him with a ten-foot frying pan," I said, and she repressed a smile. "Anyway, it isn't an act."

"You do realize that this behavior is misdirected rage at your father, don't you?" she asked.

"Mother, it has nothing to do with Dad. I don't need a hidden reason to hate El Cheapo. If you go to Florida with him instead of with me, I'll never forgive you."

"But I'm entitled to a life of my own," she said plaintively. She was probably just reciting the words of El Cheapo.

"What about me?" I asked. "Aren't I entitled to a

life? Am I supposed to lose my father and mother simultaneously?"

"Maybe you'd be happier at a boarding school," she said, "where you could have friends of your own age."

"Who suggested that? El Cheapo?"

"Stop calling him that."

I started to cry again. "I love you," I wept, "and I'm really a good true friend to you but El Cheapo is just looking for a free vacation." She sighed and got up.

"I'm going to Florida with Percy," she said. "I'm entitled to enjoy the company of someone my own age. You will go to Grandma's. After we come back, we'll talk further about your going away to school."

"Please, Mother." I was weeping now. "Take me to Florida with you. I never go anywhere. I'm bored."

"You have no right to be bored at your age."

"What's that supposed to mean?" I continued to sob noisily.

"You have your whole life ahead of you," she said. "You'll have a husband or friends to go to Florida with. But I may never get to Florida again."

"Please, Mother, couldn't the three of us go? I

wouldn't bother you. Couldn't El Cheapo pay for himself? It used to be just you and me against the world. Now it's you and him against me. There's nobody on my side."

My mother is basically tenderhearted. "Please don't cry anymore, dear," she said, putting her arms around me. "I love you very much, and I like to be with you, but I have a romantic image of this Florida vacation, and I need an escort for that—eating dinners in fancy restaurants, drinking wine with a man."

"I could lie next to the pool all day and not bother you," I said. But I knew it was no use. I tried another tack. "How come you could send me to boarding school if you can't afford to take me to Florida?"

"Grandma wants to do that for you," she said.

The thought comforted me, a little. Boarding school sounded pretty exciting. Maybe there was something to look forward to, after all.

Let me give you a little background to this whole school situation. My mother found our local high school appalling because the speech patterns were so bad. She and Percy shared a secret dream, to be mistaken for British people. They were incredible snobs. They seemed to regard grammatical errors as personal affronts. Two of the songs that I used to listen to just drove them wild. One had the words "Who done it, who stole my baby" and the other ended with "I believe in miracles, because of you and I." They would clutch their heads in horror whenever they heard these songs. "Who shall I turn to" also distressed them.

My mother was given to telling and retelling a pointless story about how one of her students had asked her if she were English. "Imagine," she'd say, "grammatical speech sounded foreign to her."

Remember *My Fair Lady?* Well, Mother and Percy were as rigid as Professor Higgins but unlike him, they would not have helped Eliza Doolittle improve her grammar. They would have cheerfully flunked her.

They would get as indignant as Henry Higgins whenever they discussed the speech at our local high school. My mother was familiar with it because most of the high school's graduates just crossed the street after graduation and attended the local college. My mother's theory was that no other college would accept them because they couldn't speak English; they spoke, as she put it, the quaint, local patois.

I wish I could give you an accurate idea of the way the kids in our high school talked. To begin with, nobody talked much. The teachers barked and the kids answered in reluctant monosyllables. Honestly, I don't think I ever heard a complete sentence in school.

"What's happenin'?" was as long a communication as one person gave to another and I never knew how to answer that aimless question.

If a boy wanted to flirt with you, he'd sidle up to your locker and say, "Where've ya bin?" You would answer with one word, "Around." Emboldened, he would ask, "Busy Saturday?" You might answer, "Babysitting." Discouraged, he'd mumble, "See ya," and the romantic dialogue would end.

My mother had taken me to see a production of *Cyrano* at the college and I could certainly see Roxanne's point of view.

In my high school, anyone who could speak well soon learned to conceal the fact, or else you were dubbed a faggot. They would have had a field day with Percy. He'd have had to leave town.

My mother was so concerned that I would adopt local speech patterns that she had been talking about private school for years, but because she had never before wanted to be alone with Percy, she had never before tried to find the money for it. My grandparents didn't like Percy (who did?) but that wasn't why they agreed to pay the school bill. They wanted to send me to boarding school because they felt bad about my being an only child. They thought I needed "peer interaction." But I didn't mind being an only child; in fact, I didn't think much about it. I saw other kids in school but when I got home it was pleasant to have the TV all to myself. However, I was quite willing to go to boarding school. I like new experiences and I figured it must be good if it cost four thousand dollars a year.

Guess what happened next. My mother took me with her to Florida. Don't think she had an attack of conscience. What really happened was that she broke up with Percy just in time. This is why.

She had to go into New York City one day to see a publisher about a possible book project. The publisher was taking her out to lunch. Going into New York City was one of my mother's favorite occupations. She said it helped her endure her expatriate life upstate. The reason she didn't go there every second day was that it was too expensive; round-trip bus fare was over thirteen dollars. And if she drove, gas, tolls, and parking would cost even more than that. Anyway, she couldn't drive because we had a neurotic car that automatically broke down any time it was more than five miles from home. This day, to her delight, the publisher was covering her travel expenses.

She had a couple of hysterical fits before she left, about how she had nothing to wear for lunch in New York City and about how she was putting on weight, and that her hair wasn't right and her nails were bitten and her purse didn't match and how out of touch with the chic life she was and on and on.

"For heaven's sake, Mother," I said, "the publisher didn't invite you for those reasons. He's interested in your mind."

That cheered her up. She gave me a hug, drove me to school, and said she'd park the car at the bus station. She didn't know what time she'd be home, "I think I'll surprise Percy," she said. I agreed to take the school bus home even though I hated it. But I was glad to take it this day because she was kind of excited and happy once she got past her appearance jitters.

I got home from school, fixed a TV dinner and a salad, and got into her blissfully empty bed to watch

(one)

TV for the rest of the evening. I assumed she'd arrive home long after I had gone to sleep.

But I was wrong. I heard the car coughing up the driveway at about ten. At first, I was so busy watching TV that I didn't look at her. It took me a minute to realize that she was crying. My mother crying? That surprised me.

"Didn't he like the book?" I asked, patting her shoulder during the commercial.

"Yes, yes," she sighed dramatically. "He liked it. He loved it."

"So why are you crying?"

"I don't want to tell you."

"Come on Mom. The show's going to start again in a minute. Tell me what's wrong."

"I can't fit it into a commercial break," she moaned. At first I considered asking her to wait until after the program, but she'd made me too nervous. I turned it off.

"It's Percy," she sobbed. I hid my joy. Maybe he had died. I put on a big anxious act.

"What about Percy?"

"He's unfaithful."

"You mean with you?" I asked.

"No," she sobbed, "I mean to me."

My God. How wonderful. Percy was going with someone else.

"It's a Captain's Paradise," she sobbed. Not only was Percy going with someone else. He was living with someone else.

Thinking that she'd be greeted by him with rapturous joy, my mother had taken the subway down to Greenwich Village after her luncheon appointment, to surprise him. She assumed he would be home because he was always talking about his long hours of slaving away over his magnum opus in his "garret." And he was home. But not alone.

"A girl named Barbara," my mother sobbed. "A girl. Can you imagine?—a girl. She didn't look much older than you. She lives there. 'Oh,' she said when Percy was forced to introduce us, 'so you're the colleague he works with on weekends.' She was very pleasant. She asked me to stay for dinner."

"Who pays for the food there?" I broke in.

"She sounded like a wife," my mother continued. "She said she'd told Percy that they should reciprocate my hospitality but he had informed her that ours was purely a work relationship."

"What nerve!" I said angrily. "Was that little creep embarrassed?"

"He wasn't the slightest bit embarrassed, or apologetic. He said, with that superior smirk of his, 'Most of our friends phone before dropping in.'" Then he walked outside with me and had the gall to ask if I would still be expecting him this weekend."

"Incredible," I said. "Mom, you should have let me hit him with the frying pan."

She ignored me and continued: "Then he started to make everything my fault. 'Just what did you expect me to do during the week?' he asked. 'Why should I be alone just because you live upstate? Anyway, we're not married. We should each have many friends. Do I stop you from having friends? I'm afraid, Althea, there is a streak of the narrow in you.'

"He had the nerve to ask me if I realized how much he'd spent to get here each weekend. He said he could have spent the same money to stay in the city and go to chamber music concerts. And he said I had no appreciation of the fact that he'd put up with you."

"You should have let me nick him a little bit, at least," I said.

"All this time," she said, weeping, "he was using me. I believed him when he told me he only liked older women. He said older women were like fine wines—they need aging. And all the time, living with a twenty-year-old. I'll bet she was one of his students. It's just like your father all over again. I need therapy. I need a psychoanalyst to tell me why I am attracted to men who are attracted to students. I want to examine my neurotic patterns."

"Please, Mom. There's nothing wrong with you. Why should you see an analyst if Percy lives with a student? Percy should see the analyst. Mom, I never liked Percy and neither did anybody else. You should be glad to be rid of him. Now maybe you'll meet someone else, someone better. Maybe you should stay away from professors. Find someone who doesn't have girl students."

She burst out laughing.

"What's funny?" I asked.

"You're funny," she said. She laughed until tears ran down her face. Suddenly she remembered. Florida was six days away. "Looks like you're going to Florida," she said.

The next day my mother and I went downtown after school. She bought me a tennis racket, a tennis outfit, a bathing suit, a dress, a shirt, and a pair of white slacks.

"How're you going to pay for this, Mom?" I asked.

"We'll stop buying food on weekends," she grinned.

The Percy episode was over.

(*two*)

I loved

the plane trip to Florida. The airline served free champagne. It wasn't great but it wasn't bad. And I loved eating on the plane. My mother's prize included first-class seats, and they kept shoving food at us from the minute we took off. The thing I loved best was the little envelope of macadamia nuts. It was the first time I had tasted them.

My mother was still brooding about Percy. He'd called her to make final plans for the trip and he was really surprised that he wasn't going. He said he was disappointed in her for going back on her word, after he'd gone to all the trouble of having his classes covered.

"Can you imagine?" she said. "He said he was glad he had found out in time about my selfish, narrow streak, that a really big person does not retaliate, and that even if I had misunderstood the situation in New York City, it did not excuse my behavior. 'If you'll forgive the cliché, Althea, two wrongs do not make a right.' He also quoted, 'Love does not alter when it alteration finds.' He said I was a great disappointment to him."

"I'll bet," I said. "He probably thought you'd feed him forever."

"He said I was being most unfair to you because you need a male figure in the household."

"Some male figure," I said. "That pipsqueak?"

"I thought he loved me," she said sadly.

"Mother," I answered, "face it. The only person Percy loves is Percy. I don't know how you put up with him for so long."

"Jen, darling," she said, "it's a fact of life that there aren't enough men to go around, and I don't want to be alone. Any man is better than no man."

"Excluding Percy."

She laughed. "Well, you certainly are consistent in your hates."

I leaned back in my seat. I had grabbed a bunch of magazines and was stuffing myself with food and plowing through the magazines, feeling really great. They were magazines that my mother and Percy wouldn't have had in the house (the only nonprofessional journal to which my mother subscribed was *The New York Review of Books*). Here were *Vogue, Harper's Bazaar, Time, People,* and *Newsweek.* I was devouring them when I suddenly realized that my mother was speaking to a man across the aisle from her. I looked at him and stifled a groan.

Sam was a diamond salesman with an apartment on Park Avenue and a condominium in Florida. He had a wife and six grandchildren. He showed my mother pictures of his grandchildren.

Sam was as gross as Percy was petite. Percy was flabby and little, Sam was flabby and fat. Sam's backside and stomach kind of oozed over all of his seat, like Jello searching for a mold. He was almost bald, and what hair he had was waxen and white. But he was beautifully dressed in a sarfari suit and had a magnificent leather attaché case. From the way he talked to the stewardesses, I could see that he did not find traveling the unusual experience we did.

Nevertheless, he did not seem nearly as smug as Percy was. Sam was loud but hesitant, booming but somehow vulnerable. I felt sorry for him. He and my mother were engaging in that chitchat called flirting. I don't know why she had to start acting girlish with that grandfather. I can't stand it when my mother gets that way—hesitant, coy, blushing, attentive, trying to please. I'm never going to act that way with men. If they don't like me the way I am, that's just too bad. I'm going to be like *Cyrano*. I won't fawn and bow and scrape and bend the knee for any man, or any woman, for that matter.

Here was another creep, richer and fatter than Percy but still a creep, and my mother was ignoring Sam's loud and unrefined voice and acting as if she'd found romance. And while Sam was twinkling at my mother, his wife was probably home watching over the grandchildren. Sam kept trying to catch my eye and smile at me, but I kept avoiding his glance. After those awful months with Percy, all I wanted was to be alone with my mother.

"Sam has offered to take us to dinner tonight," my mother said gaily. "Isn't that wonderful?"

"We don't need dinner," I reminded her. "All our meals are paid for."

Sam rocked with laughter as if I had said something brilliantly funny. His laughter reminded me of the canned laughter on TV shows. "Some sense of humor," he boomed. "But let me tell you, there's food and then again there's food. Where I'm taking you, you'll have real food."

"I want fake food," I said to my mother. "I'm not going."

"Don't be rude," she said in an angry whisper.

She took my hand and dragged me to the ladies' room. It was pretty crowded with the two of us in there.

"Are you starting again?" she asked. "What is the matter with you? A nice gentleman offers to take us to dinner and you make a big drama out of it. Why?"

"I don't like his looks," I said, "and besides, I want the two of us to be by ourselves."

"There's nothing wrong with his looks. And you will have plenty of time alone with me. So try to be enthusiastic."

"All right," I said. I really had no alternative.

We arrived at the beautiful Americana Hotel. My mother and Percy had joked about Miami Beach when they thought they were going there together, as if they would be slumming. They said it represented the worst "arriviste" tendencies in our society. But, as usual, they didn't know what they were talking about. Our room was gorgeous, big and spacious, with a closet for each of us and a double bathroom, so that if one person was using the toilet, the other person could wash up at the sink outside. And we had a marvelous view of the ocean.

We put on bathing suits and went to stretch out by the pool. A beach boy gave us big, fluffy towels to spread under us on the chaise longues, and we covered each other with suntan lotion. The sun felt like warm honey. And things kept happening. First they announced a cha-cha contest, then Bingo, and then that a woman would be walking around showing guests how to use makeup.

My mother and I giggled like two little girls when the makeup lady got to us. She was spectacular-looking, every part of her bronzed. Her blonde hair was in perfect order. I hoped my mother realized she couldn't turn out looking like the makeup lady, but she did look pretty gleaming when the makeup lady finished with her.

"Now, how about your sister?" the woman said, turning to me. Honestly, how dumb did she think we were?

"I wouldn't ruin my skin with that crap," I said rudely.

My mother tried to mask my rudeness. "She

doesn't mean that," she said, pretending to chuckle, "she's always joking."

I lay back and put my beach hat over my face. Why does my mother do things like that? Why was she apologizing to the makeup lady?

My mother decided to purchase one each of the items that had been applied to her face.

"Now, if you sign here, this will be billed to your room," the woman said.

My mother gasped. "Forty-five dollars?" she said, horrified.

"Yes," the woman said, deftly sweeping up the signed form, "everyone is amazed at how low our prices are; far lower than Revlon or Estée Lauder. We can afford to charge less because we bring the makeup directly to you. We have no overhead and we pass that saving along to you." She glided away from us.

My mother seemed really upset. "You should be happy she doesn't have an overhead," I said seriously.

My mother laughed. "Oh, well, it's done and there's no point in brooding. Sometimes I get awfully tired of being poor."

"Come on," I said, jumping up, "let's go walking on the beach."

(*two*)

The beach was wonderful. I jumped and whooped and ran and dashed and laughed and collected shells in my hat. The water was warm and embracing. At first my mother didn't want to go in the water because of her new makeup, but when she saw what a good time I was having, she changed her mind. She bobbed around with me just like another kid. I thought, this is the best fun I have ever had in my life. It's not really swimming. It's bobbing and jumping over the waves, kind of an adventure. The feeling was like nothing else. That night, as I fell asleep, I could still feel the movement of the current sweeping back and forth across my legs.

Sam picked us up in his white Cadillac. I played with the push buttons for the windows all the way to the restaurant. I felt pretty grand. It was the first time I had been in a Cadillac. My mother and Percy used to sneer at people in Cadillacs, but it was fun being in one. And I didn't have to worry about its breaking down, the way our old car always did.

We drove until we got to Key Biscayne, a narrow strip of land with water on both sides. The restaurant was called the Rusty Pelican. Outside it didn't look like much, but inside it was interesting. It reminded me of a Somerset Maugham South Sea story with fishnets and torches all over the place. All the windows looked out on the water. The people in Miami really go in for views. I like that.

"Jen," Sam boomed, "you can have anything on the menu."

"Really?"

"Absolutely," he said. "The sky's the limit."

"O.K.," I said, "I'm going to try things I've never had before. I'd like a banana frozen daiquiri, snails, a caesar salad, sweet and sour chicken, and chocolate cheese cake."

"You're too young to drink," my mother said. "They won't serve you."

"Nonsense," Sam boomed. "You're only young once. They'll serve anything I order."

The waitress only smiled and dimpled at his order. It's interesting: Nobody asks kids for their I.D.'s if they're with big spenders.

The banana daiquiri was absolutely beautiful. It came in a glass the size of the one-dollar sundae in Stewart's ice-cream parlor back home, and it looked like an ice cone. I love things made in blenders. I tasted it tentatively at first, then started to slurp. It was delicious, like a tangy banana. As far as I could see, it wasn't making me the slightest bit drunk. I ordered another and finished that one too. Then came the food.

I had never had snails before but I had learned the name *escargots* in my French class and I was curious about them. They have these little black bodies stuffed into shells. You have to use a tiny fork to get the bodies out, then you dip the bodies in garlic butter. So mostly what you're tasting is a little rubbery thing that tastes like garlic. It may sound sort of disgusting but it actually tastes very good. Then you dip up the remaining butter sauce with bread. My mother ordered something else that sounds pretty disgusting, frog's legs. They were interesting, but they couldn't compare with my snails.

I had also never eaten caesar salad before. I ordered it only because of reading *Julius Caesar* in school. It took two waiters just to make the salad. One handed the ingredients to the other, just like two doctors operating. The first one rubbed a wooden bowl with a clove of garlic and a piece of lemon. Then he filled the bowl with cut-up pieces of different kinds of lettuce, broke a raw egg over them, shook on salt, and used a gigantic pepper grinder. Then he tossed the whole thing, sprinkled on bits of bacon, tossed it again, and put in a couple of thin, flat, fishy things called anchovies. It was pretty good. My mother and Sam shared it with me because I was getting full. I was amazed at how many foods there are in the world that you just never hear about unless you go to expensive restaurants. I mean, living where I do, the only food you become an expert on is pizza.

I liked the main course, but what I have to describe is the beautiful cheese cake. It was at least six inches high—beautiful, creamy white, with chocolate marbled through it. I ate every bit of it, except for the taste I let my mother have. Then we sat around while Sam and my mother had a liqueur called kahlua which tasted like very sweet coffee.

Back at the hotel, Sam walked into the lobby with us. "I'll wait for you," he said.

"I'm a little tired," my mother said.

"Nonsense," he boomed. "The night is young. Get her settled and hurry back down. I don't like waiting."

Aha! Maybe Sam wasn't such a jovial type after all. In the elevator I could see that my mother was upset. "What's the matter?" I asked.

"Nothing," she mumbled.

(*two*)

"Mom, quick," I said when the elevator stopped, "I'm going to be sick."

She fumbled with the key opening the door, and I didn't think I could make it, but when she opened the door I dashed like a bullet to the bathroom. I was sick and I was sick.

"Oh, Mom," I moaned, as she held my head between gasps, "and it was so expensive."

The phone screamed. "I forgot all about him," my mother said.

I could hear her talking.

"I'm very sorry," she said, "but I can't leave her." She was getting angry. "Why would I make up something like that? Do you want to hear her retching? No, it's no use waiting. I'm going to put her to bed and stay with her. Tomorrow night? I don't know. We'll see how she feels." She banged down the receiver.

My mother cleaned up the mess and ran a bath for me. The hotel had bath-salt samples in the room. They smelled so good that they really aired out the room. When I got out of the bath I put on my pajamas and got into bed. My mother turned on the color TV. It was much better than the one we have at home. I felt pretty peaceful.

(*49*)

"Mom," I asked, "did you say we got free food here?"

She nodded.

"I'm hungry," I said.

"You're incredible," she said with a laugh. But she let me dial Room Service.

I ordered normal food, the kind I never threw up after: a hamburger, potato chips, and a Coke. "I'm sorry I spoiled your fun," I said.

"You didn't," she said. "I didn't want to spend any more time with him anyway, but I was afraid to hurt his feelings. It's a long time since anyone's taken me out to dinner. Before we were married, your father and I never had money for fancy meals, and we certainly didn't after we were married. But Sam's spending makes me a little uncomfortable, as if I'm taking and not giving."

"Listen, Mom, he's another creep. He should pay a lot more for the pleasure of eating with you and your absolutely divine daughter who is so appreciative of exotic food."

When my first Room Service came, I hid in the bathroom because I was in my pajamas. A little table was set up with a rose in a vase in the middle of it and the hamburger under a big metal cover to keep it warm. "Pretty classy," I said.

(two)

Then Mother and I watched an old Vincent Price horror movie, *The Fall of the House of Usher*. We spent the rest of the evening hugging each other and screaming when we got scared. It was one of the best evenings I could remember.

We were awakened the next morning by a bell-hop who brought in a vase filled with long-stemmed red roses. It was the first time we had received flowers, although I'd seen many expensive-looking flower boxes delivered in the old movies I watched on TV. Percy had once brought my mother "one perfect rose" and somehow convinced her that this was in better taste than a whole vase full of roses. Naturally, that was just Percy's rationalization for his cheapness. Me, I'll take the whole vulgar vase-ful, anytime.

The card that came with the flowers said that Sam hoped I was feeling better. He wanted us to have dinner again that night. If he didn't hear from us, he'd automatically pick us up at six. Under the circumstances it seemed ungracious not to go.

"Why do you think he's so anxious to see us?" I asked my mother.

"I think he's lonely," she said. "Isn't it possible that he's just looking for some pleasant company?"

"You can hardly call me pleasant company," I

said. "And it's funny that if he has a home here, he doesn't have lots of friends already. Do you think he could be interested in you, you know, romantically?"

"Of course not. We just met, had one dinner, and you're already fantasizing. He's just being hospitable. Maybe he's being kind because he knows this is our first time here."

"I'd rather be alone with you," I said. "You could have someone take the flowers back and say we've left town."

"Why should we?" she asked. "It's kind of nice to know someone here."

"Then would you mind if I don't go with you to dinner?" I asked. "I'd rather have Room Service again and watch one of the movies they advertise. You know, the movies you call the operator for, and they bill it to your room. There's one called *Little Girl in the Rain* that sounds interesting."

"Of course, darling," she said. "It's your vacation, too. If you're sure you won't be lonely, it's fine with me."

Since neither of us had ever done it before, we decided to go deep-sea fishing that day. The hotel said they would prepare any fish that we caught for us to eat. I was excited. We had read Hemingway's *The Old Man and the Sea* in school, and I had seen a lot of movies about the sea. As we moved out of the dock, I was enchanted with the beauty of the water. But this too turned out like some of our other adventures, not so special.

To begin with, fishing is boring. If only I had thought to bring a book. A lot of tourists who didn't know each other were stationed along the edges of an old tub, sitting at fishing rods that were fixed into holes. When one of the rods started to shake, a mate ran over and helped the tourist reel in a fish. There didn't seem to be much skill associated with it. How can people refer to fishing like this as a sport? It's just plain dumb luck, and I guess I was getting irritated because none of that dumb luck was coming my way. The people on the opposite side of the boat kept catching groupers, but nothing even nibbled at the bait on our side.

Finally, my mother gave up and lay down on a corner of the deck. "At least I can get a sunburn," she said. I sat on at my post, miserable but determined not to despair.

I did despair when lunch came. The boat's brochure said lunch was included, so we didn't bring anything to supplement their lunch. What a mistake! Lunch consisted of cold bologna sandwiches on wet bread with mustard dripping from it. As a drink, we had warm orange soda pop. They didn't even have coffee for my mother.

We were also unaware of how the Florida weather can change without warning. Suddenly the seas got rough, and we got cold. Other passengers had been smart enough to bring warm jackets, but all we had were thin little windbreakers, which when we'd bought them had seemed most appropriate for Florida. Finally, I gave up fishing. Hemingway could keep it. My mother and I huddled together to keep warm while the boat pitched and rocked. I was still feeling queasy from the previous night and now Mother, too, looked kind of green.

"No wonder they gave us this vacation as a gift," she groaned.

I laughed, miserable as I was.

We were supposed to stay out until five o'clock, but when a light rain began, the captain turned the boat around and headed for shore. We just sat there with our teeth chattering.

"Do they know something I don't know?" my mother asked, looking at the other passengers, who seemed to be having fun.

"They're drinking beer," I said. "Do you want some?"

This time it was my mother's turn to be sick. Poor thing, she said she had thrown up only once before in her life, when she was pregnant. As we stepped out onto the dock, she could hardly stand. A taxi took us back to the hotel, and she crawled into bed and stayed there.

When Sam called she was fast asleep. I went down to the lobby to explain things to him.

"She's not avoiding me, is she?" he boomed.

"Oh, no," I said, "she wouldn't do anything like that."

"Well, little lady, would you like to have dinner with me?" he asked.

I hesitated, but he seemed so lonely and disappointed that I said, "Sure." He reminded me somewhat of my grandfather.

I ran upstairs to tell my mother and she seemed relieved that we would both be occupied for the evening. Sam decided that we should stay in the hotel, so he took me into the Gaucho Room. It was a pretty room, but so dark that I could hardly read the menu. A lot of Florida's restaurants are like that. The more expensive they are, the darker they are. You'd think it would be just the opposite, that cheap restaurants would keep things dark so you couldn't see the food.

I seemed to have recovered completely from the previous night's sickness. I ordered shrimp cocktail, a steak, a salad with Roquefort dressing, a baked potato with sour cream and chives, broccoli, and profiteroles. Profiteroles are little cream puffs filled with ice cream and covered with chocolate sauce. Everything was great, but I was worried about how expensive it all was.

"Don't you mind spending all this money?" I asked.

"I'm putting you on my expense account, little lady," Sam replied.

"Why do you call me little lady?"

"I've forgotten your name," he said honestly.

I laughed and told him. He wanted me to call him Sam even though he was a grandfather. "Do you have pictures of your grandchildren?" I asked.

"What grandfather doesn't?" He laughed. "But generally people get bored."

"I'd love to see them," I said.

"You're not just being polite?" He hesitated.

"No, honest. I like big families. Don't think I'm complaining. It's O.K. to be an only child, you get all of the attention, and my mother couldn't afford to support more than me, but it's kind of lonesome around Christmas and holidays."

"I don't like New Year's Eve myself," he boomed. "Big waste of time and money."

"I like New Year's Eve," I said. "I like to watch TV when that ball in Times Square is descending. My mother attaches a special kind of importance to New Year's Eve. She says it's a carryover from when she was a girl. Then you absolutely didn't rate if you didn't have a date on New Year's Eve. I certainly don't look forward to this New Year's Eve, without my father. My mother says it will be her first one without a date in her whole life."

"How do you know your father won't be back by then?" he asked.

"He has leave until the end of spring semester of next year," I said. "So my mother will be lonely."

"I'm always lonely on New Year's Eve," he said.

"How can you be lonely with your big family? Don't they all pay you homage as the family patriarch?"

He laughed. "The only one who pays is me," he said. "I pay and they get, all year long. New Year's Eve is no exception."

"I wish somebody was around to pay for us," I said.

"Does your mother feel that way?" He asked, interested.

"Oh, absolutely. She once said she'd sell her soul to be rid of debts. She's always worrying about money."

"But she teaches at a college, doesn't she?"

"Sure."

"Doesn't she get paid?"

"Teaching college isn't the same as selling diamonds," I said. "She's an associate professor at a small college and makes very little money. And my father can't help us either, because he's on leave without pay."

Then he asked me all about my father. Feeling a little disloyal, I told him the story.

"Do you hear from him?" Sam asked.

"I just got a postcard," I said. "He said he loved me and looked forward to seeing me next spring."

Sam asked me if my mother was going to get a divorce, and I said I really didn't know what she intended to do. This was true. As open as my mother and I were with each other, we never discussed my father. I thought she was still too badly hurt to want to be reminded of it.

"I think what she'd like to do," I said, "would be to get a job somewhere else so she wouldn't be embarrassed any longer. She'd love to live in Florida. She really likes it here."

"Do you really think she'd like to live in Florida?" Sam asked.

"Absolutely," I said. "This is the first time she's ever been here, and she wouldn't even be here if she hadn't won the trip. New Paltz is an okay town in the summer, but in winter it's all snow and slush. We never know when our temperamental car is going to break down and leave us freezing."

We had finished dinner. We walked to the house phone and Sam called my mother. He had to be out of town on business for the next two days, but he asked her to dinner on the night he'd be back and thanked her for letting me join him tonight. Then he asked her if he might buy me a little memento of Florida. She said it would be all right as long as it wasn't too expensive a gift.

The shops in that hotel are open even at night. Sam took me to the beach shop and bought me a matching hat and beach bag.

"Should you be spending all this money?" I asked.

"Don't you worry," he said. "This isn't real money. Plenty more where this came from."

I wished he was my grandfather. What a pleasure not to have to count pennies.

After we finished shopping, Sam seemed to have nothing to do with himself. "I don't think I'm quite ready to go home and watch television," he said. "Would you like to go to a movie?"

I felt sorry for him, but I was too tired to go anywhere. He walked me to the elevator and stood there. I got into the elevator, looked back out at him, waved, and felt sad. He had a big family and plenty of money, but he looked lonely and vulnerable standing there.

"Mom," I asked when I got to the room, "why would a man with a wife and six grandchildren and two homes and a Cadillac and lots of money be lonesome?"

"Everyone's lonesome," she said.

"Even married people?"

"Everyone. You can be lonesome outside a marriage and inside a marriage. It's kind of natural to be lonesome at times. After all, we are each really alone, under our own skins."

"So what can we do?"

"Accept it. That's what I do. Instead of saying, 'I'm lonely,' I say, 'Isn't it great that tonight I'll be alone and have plenty of time to wash my hair.'"

I thought about being lonely a long time before I fell asleep. Maybe my watching TV so much was my way of not feeling lonesome.

The next day it rained. We rented a car and went to Marineland. I enjoyed seeing how smart dolphins can be, but I also thought it was sad to see those big things jumping through hoops. It was kind of undignified. I don't like the idea that you can get them to do just about anything by offering them food. I found myself wishing that every one of those dolphins could get out and roam the ocean, but I knew that wouldn't do them much good either. I had read that Japanese fishermen were killing dolphins along with the tuna catch. Maybe, someday, if people could really communicate with dolphins, we could find out if they'd rather be fed and taken care of and forced to do silly tricks, or whether they'd prefer to take their chances along with freedom.

"If this rain keeps up, we won't have a sunburn," my mother said. "If the sun comes out tomorrow, I'm going to spend the entire day lying by the pool. I want to go home with one of those expensive-looking sunburns."

Right after breakfast the next day, she was spread out on a chaise, her skin dripping with suntan lotion.

She kept rotating sides like a barbecuing chicken. She wouldn't even go in for lunch because the sun is apparently highest and most potent at noon.

She looked marvelous by dinner time. We had another great dinner, then went back to our room to watch television. I was awakened in the middle of the night by her groaning. She looked like a lobster.

"I warned you," I said. I spread Solarcaine all over her body, but it didn't seem to help. She groaned all night, then fell asleep near morning. By midmorning she was covered with blisters. I felt sorry for her but it didn't interfere with my fun. I swam during the day, had meals with her in our room, and watched hours of TV. The time passed too quickly. The day before we were due to leave, she finally struggled up.

"Your face looks like leprosy," I giggled.

"With friends like you, who needs enemies?" she joked. We had heard the comedian at the hotel use this line.

"I'm only being factual," I said.

She finally nerved herself to look in the mirror. She gazed at the sight in horror. "People will think I've been in a war instead of on vacation." Just then, the phone rang. "It was Sam," she said. "I just remembered that I promised to have dinner with him our last night here. But I think you and I should be alone together tonight."

"I don't mind your going out, Mom," I said. "Go and have a good time. We've been together every night but one, and we'll be together on the plane home."

That night, my mother finally struggled into her clothes. Every spot she touched was painful. But she kissed me cheerfully enough and went down to the lobby to meet Sam. I called the desk and made an after-dinner appointment to see the special movie. It was a porno film, and I fell asleep watching it. What a bore. It had nothing to do with a little girl in the rain. It was a waste of three dollars.

My mother awakened me when she came in, by turning off the TV. She seemed perturbed, paced around a bit, and looked over at me several times.

"I'm up," I said.

She lit a cigarette.

"Since when do you smoke?" I asked.

"Sam bought me a pack."

"Would you take cancer if you got it for free?" I asked.

"Jen, don't bother me now about the cigarette,"

she pleaded. "Just tell me what you told Sam about me."

"Who remembers?" I said, trying to sound like Sam. "I just made conversation. Did I say something wrong?"

"I don't know what you said," she told me. "But did you give Sam the idea that I would like to stay in Florida and was in desperate need of money?"

"I suppose I may have. I told him how little money you make. Why?" I asked.

"He told me how lonely he is all the time and offered to 'set me up' in an apartment here and pay all the expenses, just so he'd have someone to spend time with."

"That's great," I said. "I'd love to stay here. Can we?"

"Of course not," she said. "I didn't get a doctorate to end up like that."

"But, Mom," I said, "it would be great. No snow, and no worrying about that neurotic car. Maybe you could get a job here, too."

"Oh, Jen," she said with a laugh, as she rumpled my hair, "you really don't understand, do you?"

Maybe I wasn't understanding. I don't know.

"All I can say," I told her, "is that I would be perfectly satisfied to have him for a grandfather."

"You know what," she answered, "I would be perfectly satisfied to have him for a grandfather, too." Then she went into gales of laughter. Honestly, sometimes I don't understand her at all.

It was strange. Percy took from us, and Sam wanted to give to us; yet my mother preferred Percy. Whatever was wrong with Sam, he wasn't a selfish pig like Percy. I guess I really didn't understand.

(*three*)

After we

returned from Florida, my mother decided to devote herself to social welfare. She was still upset about her experience with Percy. I guess it seemed like just too much, coming so close on the heels of my father's defection. Incidentally, I received postcards from my father from time to time, but they no longer sounded chipper and optimistic.

My mother said that she wanted to expand her circle of women friends, that most of the men on campus were either homosexual, poor, or married, and that her ideal now was to achieve *agape*, which is a Greek word for love of humanity. She then started looking around for ways to practice agape.

The first thing she did was to plan a luncheon for the twenty-two women in the division in which she taught. She sent out invitations for a Saturday luncheon. Five of the women sent regrets because they were on the Tenure and Promotion Committee and thought my mother was reaching out to them only because she wanted to be promoted. My mother was mortified at this misreading of her agape intentions. Ten others had previous appointments or wanted to be with their families. Two were going shopping with their husbands. That left five for the luncheon, including my mother. You won't believe the absolute boredom of that day.

One of the women who showed up was Heloise McNitt, professor of children's literature, who was of southern origin and lived with her aged mother. When my mother brought up the question of women forging a link and supporting one another, Heloise said, "Honey, I been supportin' my mother fo' my entire life. I jest hope I live long 'nough fo' my retirement."

A second was Yolanda Clauss, professor of children's drama, who was married to a tyrant of a drama critic. She had a big beauty mark in the center of her forehead, like an Indian caste mark, and she was afraid of the sound of her own voice. "I have to leave right after we eat," she kept saying, "because Ted wants me at home this afternoon."

A third was a lecturer at the bottom of the academic heap who was soon to leave the college; the fourth was an inept Viennese lecturer on child psychology who remained seductive and interested in men, despite her rather advanced age. She kept asking my mother to introduce her to someone. "I just never meet anyone," she kept saying. I guess the women at the luncheon didn't qualify as "anyone." I didn't like her a bit and kind of wished my mother would introduce her to Percy. A few weekends of feeding that sponge would teach her not to regard women as non-persons.

It was evident that these women could not provide the basis for my mother's agape. "I don't understand it," she said after the luncheon. "On other campuses there are thriving women's groups. We just seem to be behind the times." Perhaps this was just as well, because soon a good opportunity came along for her to practice agape.

The dean asked her to teach at Walkill Prison, near the college. Actually, they don't call it a prison;

(*three*)

they call it a correctional facility. It was a minimum-security facility, and my mother was excited about the opportunity.

"Just think," she said. "I'll be the first woman to teach there."

We spent a lot of time trying to decide what she should wear for the first session. She kept talking about donning dun colored plumage; on the other hand, she didn't want it to appear as if she didn't care about looking nice for the prisoners. She ended up wearing a black sweater and skirt and a thin gold chain around her neck. She wore none of that fancy makeup from Florida.

I couldn't wait to hear about that first session. The college was offering four courses at Walkill: Black History, Sociology, Psychology, and my mother's writing course. On the first day each professor had to explain the purpose of the course to the inmates and then show why they should take a particular course.

"I didn't know what I'd say when it was my turn," my mother related. "I was a little nervous. I'd never had to sell a course that way before. I wasn't even thinking until I was standing there, and then I told them that writing was a joy, a particular human activity, that it makes one feel better to write even if the work doesn't get published. I also told them that writing helps people to get in touch with themselves, to understand themselves and their lives. Sometimes we don't even know how we feel about something until we see it in writing. Fifty men signed up for the course, but we had to limit it to twenty-five."

"How did you decide which ones to take?" I asked.

"We picked the twenty-five who were serving the longest sentences, so they will be able to finish the course."

"You picked the ones with run-on sentences," I said as a joke.

"Why, Jen," my mother said, "you're turning into a fifteen-year-old wit."

"Percy would have been proud of me," I said, crossing my eyes.

My mother loved her work at Walkill. It was a perfect place for agape. She would spend long hours every day reading her inmate students' writing. Sometimes she stayed after her class was over to observe their Daytop meetings, sessions at which they sat around talking about how they had become drug addicts. I had seen junkies in high school and thought they were pretty unappealing. But my mother got excited about them because they were a novelty.

One night she brought home a tape from a Daytop meeting. "Listen to this," she told me, her eyes glistening with tears. "I never cease to marvel at the resilience of the human spirit, at its will to survive, to endure."

She was sounding a bit like Percy, kind of flowery and phony. But she meant well, so I listened. Each of the ex-junkies told how he had embarked on his life of crime, how much misery he had caused his loved ones, and how he was going to make amends to himself, his family, and society, once he got out of jail. My mother said this confessional technique was borrowed from Alcoholics Anonymous. My mother was particularly fond of one inmate, Clarence Brown, who had been really evil and had made a total recovery. Before he was released, she gave him a book as a gift.

The next Saturday night, at two A.M., we were awakened by the phone. It was Clarence Brown's mother. My mother was indignant when she got off the phone. It seems that Clarence had been standing at a bar, minding his own business, when a policeman had entered and beaten him up, gashing his face and knocking out a tooth. Now Clarence was in jail in New York City.

"So why are they calling you?" I asked sleepily.

"They want me to go to the arraignment tomorrow," she replied. "Want to come to New York City?"

"No," I said, "I have homework. I want to watch TV, too. I thought you couldn't afford to go to New York City."

"This is an emergency."

"Tell them to call someone else."

"Don't you have any social conscience?" she asked.

"Not in the middle of the night," I said, "and not about ex-junkies."

Mother was gone by the time I got up the next day. It was Sunday so I made myself my favorite unhealthy breakfast—two bagels smeared with cream cheese, and a cup of cocoa. Then I settled down to do my homework. Next I watched a hilarious movie with Ann Sheridan and Zachary Scott, in which he goes away to World War II and she has an affair with an artist and then kills him so he won't tell her husband. When the truth is revealed, Zachary Scott says he can forgive her for the murder but not for the affair. They really had some strange ideas back then.

Suddenly I realized that it was five o'clock and I began to get worried. I calmed myself by making some dinner for Mother and me, and at six o'clock she came limping in, all bandaged up.

"My God," I shrieked, "what happened to you?"

She had gone to the arraignment and Clarence had been let off with a stern warning. The judge was apparently impressed by my mother's appearance there. Then my mother had gone home with Clarence to meet *his* mother, who had telephoned the night before. Clarence's mother has been confined to a wheelchair in recent years because of some disease.

"So what happened?" I asked.

"I walked over to her wheelchair to shake her hand. She had this big German shepherd dog guarding her. The dog sprang at me and bit me on the arm and thigh. I had to go to St. Luke's Hospital for stitches."

"Gee," I said, "that's a terrible experience. I'm sorry I wasn't with you. Was it hard driving home?"

"No," she said. "I'm not in pain. I guess the local anesthesia hasn't worn off yet."

"Are you sorry you went?" I asked.

"No," she said, "it's part of my plan for agape."

"It sounds more to me like the natives eating the missionary," I said.

She burst out laughing. "I told you you were getting witty."

My mother's social conscience was undiminished by the dog's attack. The following week I came home from school and saw a man sitting on the porch having tea with her.

"Say hello to Fred," she said.

"Hi," I said.

Fred wasn't letting me off that easily. He held out his hand and insisted on shaking mine. To tell you the truth, I hate shaking hands. I don't know why, but I feel awkward about it. I never know when to shake hands and when not to.

"This is Fred's first day of freedom," my mother said.

"Thanks to your mother, honey," he said. "She helped me to get out."

My mother had gotten the newly released Fred a scholarship to the college, a free dormitory room, and meal tickets. He was planning to major in sociology, and my mother was really pleased at the thought that she might save one person from the streets.

Fred was around our house a lot the first few weeks after his release, "making the transition back to society." I didn't really like having him there. He made me feel self-conscious. I couldn't run around half naked the way my mother and I were accustomed to doing, and with him there at dinner every night, I couldn't even talk freely to my mother.

"I should think you'd have better sense with a teen-age girl around," my grandmother said.

"Fred is a wonderful person," my mother answered, "and he'll be moving into his dorm and starting his studies within the week. There's really nothing to worry about."

I started to like Fred. He was helpful and cooperative. Every day he did something else around the house. He finished all the little home-improvement projects my father had started. He was so humble, so unlike Percy, so grateful if I even gave him a cold glass of water. This really puzzled me. I mean, here was a real-life murderer—well, he had killed a drug dealer—just like you'd read about or see in the movies, and he was a very nice person. He treated my mother politely. He never free-loaded for meals, at least not after the first week. He always brought something: two tomatoes, a head of lettuce, two cans of beer. With everything, he had a certain pride and dignity and a desire not to impose. I liked Fred very much. I didn't feel the anxiety with him that I had felt around Percy.

Once Fred got involved in his courses, however, we saw a lot less of him. He'd come up from time to time to mow the lawn or help my mother with something. I enjoyed observing someone who was handy around the house. I regretted the fact that I wasn't handy, had never really thought about home improvement, and so I liked to watch Fred work, thinking I might learn something by watching.

My mother decided to give a cocktail party to introduce Fred to people. He looked pretty spiffy in a suit and tie, all dressed up. When I saw him dressed up I realized how old he was. He was close to forty, practically as old as my mother.

My mother's colleagues were absolutely thrilled to meet him. Most of them had never even driven past a jail, so it gave them a thrill to socially meet an actual jailbird. (I know that "jailbird" is not a nice word.) And Fred just loved their interest. Over and over again he regaled them with stories of his deprived boyhood and life of crime. It was the same sort of stuff I had heard on the Daytop tape.

A bunch of effete professors, minor-league Percys, stood around him, hanging on to his every word as he explained, "You see, man, I was like crazy. I had to have it and he just stood there laughing at me. I couldn't take it, man. So I shot him."

The crowd all agreed with him that he had performed a noble function in ridding the world of a drug dealer. I mean, it was incredible. I was fond of Fred, but he was no saint and they acted as if he was. I mean, really, when you get right down to it, he was a murderer who had served his time. I thought they should have been making more of a fuss over my mother, who hadn't done anything wrong, but was, nevertheless, committed to agape.

A good period began for my mother. Our house was now always full of people on weekends. I guess I hadn't realized how powerful the silence had been after my father's departure. And my mother didn't have to worry about paying for the gatherings, either. The people who came always brought wine or cider or something to eat.

Suddenly, everyone was after Fred. The English department wanted him for a course on Black English; Sociology wanted him for Urban Education;

Education wanted him for Education of the Disadvantaged; Health Studies wanted him for Drug Guidance; and Black Studies wanted him for just about everything. At first, all these groups seemed to think it was necessary to get him through my mother.

Then, some smart hostess found out it wasn't necessary to invite my mother; overnight, she was back to being a single woman on a campus where the competition was all under thirty. The weekends grew silent again.

"What happened to Fred?" I asked her one empty weekend.

"He can't visit us," she said. "He's booked up all weekend."

"So why can't you go with him?" I asked.

"I wasn't invited."

"Well, couldn't he take you anyway?" I persisted.

"No, you can't do that. That would look as if we were going together or something like that."

"It already looks like that," I told her. "Everyone in the community thinks you're having a romance with him."

"That's nonsense," she said. "People are so narrowminded. They just don't understand agape."

I was pleased that my mother wasn't romantically

involved with Fred. Not because he was black. I like to think that I don't have any prejudices about black people. And not because he had been in jail, either. After all, the Count of Monte Cristo (I just saw that on TV with Richard Chamberlain) also spent time in jail. And not just because he killed a drug dealer, although I would be lying if I told you that I approved of that.

The big reason I was glad my mother wasn't involved with him was that somewhere out there he had a wife and two children, and according to my mother, he had made absolutely no attempt to see any of them since he'd been out of jail. There he was, a big campus celebrity, lapping it up at cocktail parties and dinners and fund-raising affairs, and his kids were out there growing up without a father. I have no use for fathers who desert their children.

So we stopped seeing Fred, although he still dropped in from time to time to say hello and to tell my mother about his accomplishments. He was now teaching two courses himself, had received straight *A*s in all the courses he was taking, and was the father confessor of his dorm.

My mother seemed a little lonely and moped around the house on weekends.

"Are you sad?" I asked her.

"Not really," she answered. "Just a bit at loose ends. It will pass. I have the satisfaction of having helped another human being."

The Friday before final exam week at the college, the phone rang. My mother answered it, talked for a few minutes, then came into the kitchen and burst into tears.

"What's wrong?" I asked nervously. It had been almost a month since I'd heard from my father and I always worried about that.

"A friend of mine who works at the bank just called. It's Freddy," she gasped. "Oh, my God, how could he do such a thing?"

"What did he do?" I asked.

It seems that Freddy had walked into the local bank, where everybody knew him, and had walked up to the cashier. The conversation went like this:

"Hello, Freddy," she said. "How's the world treating you?" She then looked up and saw a gun pointed at her across the counter.

"Sorry to do this, Graciela," he said, "but I have to ask you to hand over some money."

"Freddy," she said, "you must be joking. Quickly, put the gun away, get out of here, and I won't tell anybody."

"I can't do that," he replied gently.

Graciela said he had appeared stoned to her. He had taken $40,000. Now the police were looking for him.

"Do you think he'll come here?" I asked.

"I don't know."

"I'll lock the doors and windows," I said, jumping up.

"Don't be silly. Sit down and let me think. I hope he does come here so I can help him. Why did he do such a thing? I know that he was worried about his father, who has cancer."

"Help him!" I shrieked. "Are you out of your mind? This is carrying agape too far. I'm going to get Daddy's hunting rifle."

"Stop it," my mother gasped. "He probably won't come here, but if he does, you are going to treat him gently and not frighten him with a gun. If he saw a gun he might panic and then there's no telling what could happen."

"You mean, you want us to just sit here and wait?" I asked.

"No," she said, "you can go and do the laundry downstairs."

I was scared. If I hadn't been so scared, I would

have been having a good time. This was pretty interesting and I could see myself writing a composition about it for school or telling the kids about it and being kind of a celebrity in school because of it.

At about five o'clock I heard a car. I looked outside and it was Fred, all right, but not like you see in the movies, with bloodhounds and sheriffs and all that. He was carrying a big bag from Jumping Jack: hamburgers, malteds, tacos, apple pies, french fries. I bet he used the stolen money to buy that stuff.

"Hello Fred," my mother said. "How nice of you to bring dinner."

"Should I call the police?" I whispered as he approached.

"Not yet," she said.

I couldn't believe he had just robbed a bank. He seemed absolutely the same as usual.

"Hi, Jen," he said.

"Hi, Fred."

The three of us sat down on the porch with our snack.

"Delicious," my mother said. "I've never stopped in there but in the future I will."

The strangest thing is that we were all starved. We ate and ate until everything was gone. Then my mother sat back and looked at him.

"Why?" was all she asked.

He shook his head in bewilderment. "Would you believe me if I said I didn't know?" he answered.

"But what triggered it? Tell me," she pleaded.

"I don't know," he repeated. "I got into my car to go to my exam and suddenly I found myself in the bank. I guess you might call it a compulsion. All the time I was doing it I thought I was asleep, that it was a dream. Afterward, driving away, I suddenly realized it was no dream. I parked, got out, opened the trunk of my car, and saw all that money and the gun. I drove up in the mountains and walked around a little bit, trying to understand. Then I took a nap in the car, woke up and drove to Jumping Jack, got the food, and came up here. I thought you and Jen would be hungry, too."

"Jen," my mother said, "why don't you call College Security while we have some coffee."

I made the call and then we waited some more.

"Will you write to me?" Fred asked us.

My mother started to cry. I did too. "Of course we will," we sobbed.

Then Fred started to cry. "I guess I just couldn't face that exam," he said.

Some hardened criminal! If only he could return the money and go to class the next day, keep going to parties and being the campus celebrity. Oh, if only we could turn back time. It's so terrible that you can't change the past. If I could, I would have wished my father home and Fred safe. But there's no pretending; once something is done, there's no going back.

"I want to tell you, Althea," he said pathetically, "that nobody has ever been better to me than you. All your work to get me into college and to get me the scholarship. I'm sorry I failed you."

"Don't think about me," my mother said. "I liked helping you. It made my life richer."

"There were an awful lot of people expecting an awful lot of me," he said. "Everywhere I turned there were people, you know, pulling at me. I was afraid of disappointing everybody, you dig?"

We both dug.

A car drove up; it was the College Security car. I opened the side door to the man walking toward the house. He didn't look like my idea of a policeman. He was very handsome, about six feet three in height and with a bristling mustache and a nice smile. In his bigness and warm smile he reminded me of my father.

His name was Henrik and he was chief officer on

the college's security force. He and my mother had never met before even though they had both been on the campus for a long time. That's a funny thing about this college—the professors have nothing to do with anyone who works there, except for other teachers, until a problem arises.

"Hi, Fred," Henrik said. Then he lit a cigar and sat down with us at the kitchen table. "I'd love a cup of coffee," he told my mother.

I could feel her bristle. My mother doesn't like cops. I think she will always remember them beating kids up during the Vietnam protests on campuses; see them at Kent State, Jackson State, in Harvard Square, Grant Park, and at Berkeley. To her, they're all brutal Archie Bunkers—"pigs," like the kids used to call them.

But Henrik seemed gentle, friendly, almost a little shy. My mother was icily polite to him, but he was so nice and easy he didn't seem to notice. He just sat and drank his coffee.

"Well, Fred," he said at last, "I guess it's time to go."

Henrik did not handcuff him. I don't think I could have stood that. I ran over to Fred and gave him a kiss on the cheek. "Write to us," I said.

"I will, honey," he said. "Most of the people I've seen in my life have been mean. But you and your mother are good people. I'm sorry I let you down."

My mother and I clung to each other weeping after Henrik collected the bank's money and drove off with Fred. He'd told us they'd be around later on to collect Fred's car. You can't imagine how empty the house felt.

"Can I sleep in your bed tonight?" I asked.

She nodded, crying so hard she couldn't speak.

"I guess agape can be pretty painful," I said.

She nodded again, still crying. "What a waste, what a waste," she said over and over again.

"I don't think I can sleep tonight," she said.

"Me, neither."

So we watched television through the Late Late Show and the next thing I knew it was morning and we had fallen asleep with the TV on. And there were all the familiar cartoons of my childhood waking us up. They were all jolly and funny and safe. They reminded me of a much simpler time.

The events of the night before started to evaporate, like a bad dream. You know what I mean. Sometimes you have a bad dream and the next day

(*three*)

you feel vaguely upset but can't remember exactly
what caused your bad feeling. That's how it was all
through Saturday. We mooned around and couldn't
seem to get ourselves organized. Only late in the
day did we begin the Saturday routine of cleaning
the house. And bit by bit we felt better.

(*four*)

Henrik started

to visit us at the house. The first time he came to pick up Fred's car. My mother was cold to him but she was anxious to talk about Fred.

"Why do you think he did it?" she asked Henrik.

"He wanted to be caught, to go back to jail," he answered.

"Nonsense," said my mother, the big authority on criminals. "Nobody wants to go back to jail. He must have needed the money desperately. Maybe because his father was sick."

"He wanted to get caught," Henrik insisted.

"That's why he went to a bank where everybody knew him."

"What a waste," my mother said.

"It was a waste of our time, that's for sure," said Henrik.

She cast him a baleful look but it just went right past him. I guess cops are accustomed to dealing with this kind of thing. "I didn't mean a waste of time for you," she snapped. "I meant a waste of his life, a waste for him to be back in jail."

"Maybe so," he said soberly, "but maybe that's the best place for him."

"He could have been saved," my mother persisted.

"You're wrong," Henrik said. "That should be obvious to you. Didn't you try? Didn't everyone? Some people can be saved, and some can't and some shouldn't be saved."

"Well," she said huffily, "that's the attitude I'd expect from a cop."

"I'm not a cop," he smiled. She couldn't ruffle him. "I'm a security officer."

"Same difference."

"No, it isn't. I'm not qualified to be a cop. I wasn't trained for it."

"What were you trained for, if anything?" she

asked. Come on Mom. He's so nice. Don't be so haughty. How about agape for him?

"Nothing much," he said humbly. "I'm going to the community college now, trying to get my degree in police science. My main interest, however, is music."

"Music," my mother said. "Do you mean rock and roll?"

"Classical music," he said. "I get over to Tanglewood a couple of times every summer."

My mother sat back and looked at him, deflated. But after that, they began to get friendly.

Henrik and my mother seemed to have nice vibrations between them. Nothing heavy, the way there was with Percy. I wasn't even sure that this was a romance. It seemed more like just friendship. My mother would sit and talk to Henrik by the hour, just the way I would with a school friend.

It gave me a warm feeling to come home from school and see that official Security car parked in our driveway. I felt protected with a man around the house again. I know that my father never really protected us from anything, but I had felt a lot safer when my father had been home. Now I felt protected again with Henrik.

(four)

There was none of the conflict that had existed between Percy and me. I never had the feeling that Henrik was taking my mother away from me. He never seemed to resent me, to want me out of the room. And of course Henrik never slept over, so he didn't deprive me of color TV.

Neither Henrik nor my mother had any money, so they never went anywhere. They just kind of sat around being peaceful together. I think his friendship was good for my mother; it calmed her and made her more secure. Henrik told her about court cases, crimes, his own research; and he showed her a side of campus life that she had previously never even thought about.

"Mom," I asked her one day, "are you in love with Henrik?"

"I'm very fond of him," she said. "If you mean do we have a romantic attachment, the answer is no."

"Why not?"

"Just not."

"Were you in love with Percy?"

"I think so."

"How could you be in love with Percy and not with Henrik?"

"Honey, please drop the subject," she said. Then,

turning away, she added, "Henrik didn't even finish college."

"So what? I think he's a great human being. He's a lot better than some of those phony English professors you know."

She was getting mad. "Look, let's drop Henrik and Percy. Let's talk about *your* boy friends."

"Ha, ha, very funny. You know I don't have any."

"Well, when you do you'll find that you don't like my interference."

"I probably won't have any until I'm too old to do anything with them."

"Darling, be patient. You'll find love soon enough."

"How will I know when I'm in love?" I asked.

"You just will. It's something that happens without volition."

"And you can't make yourself love Henrik?"

"No."

"Or not love Percy?"

Her eyes looked watery. "No."

"Are you telling me that a person has absolutely no control over love?" I looked at her with wonder.

"None at all."

"How awful," I gasped. "It sounds kind of like a

disease or a plague from heaven."

"Or a gift from heaven," my mother said.

"Let me get this clear." I thought for a minute. "You kind of wait around for love to strike, like in *Romeo and Juliet*?"

"Exactly."

"But suppose love never strikes? Then what can people do?"

"They do without, they settle, they lie to themselves, they pretend, they think that by adopting love's postures they will actually find themselves in love."

"Does that happen to many people?"

"I'm afraid so."

"Well, if they don't *know* they aren't in love, maybe it doesn't seem so bad."

"Maybe."

"Still," I mused, "it doesn't seem fair. Some people just live and other people love them, and some people never get loved. It's kind of like some people are born with musical talent, or sports talent. And some people are born with love talent."

"Right."

"Can even rich and beautiful people not have love?"

"Yes."

"And an ugly, unimportant person can?"

"Sure."

It seemed pretty scary and chancy to me. Sort of like playing Bingo. I thought for a moment, then asked, "Isn't it possible that someone might find love in one place and not in another? I mean, you might not find love here, but you might find it in New York City?"

"That's right." She laughed. "That's why people travel. It's the basis of the tourist business."

I giggled. "You mean people don't really go to see famous churches?"

"Only secondarily."

She seemed so positive. Of course, she hadn't done much traveling, so maybe she didn't know. But it was true that my father had gone off to Denmark with his student. Why Denmark? Why couldn't he have stayed here, near me?

"Let me get this straight," I said. "Love just hits you, like in *Romeo and Juliet,* and there's nothing you can do to get it."

"Yes, that's my opinion. But I'm not exactly the world's greatest authority on love. In fact, you might well describe it as one of my failure areas."

Her mood was changing. I didn't mean to make her feel depressed.

"Why are you asking me all these questions?" she asked.

"I don't want to upset you," I said cautiously. "I'm just trying to find out. I mean, kids in school talk a lot about getting laid, but nobody seems to understand anything about being in love."

She reached out and hugged me, cheerful again. "All right, what else do you want to know?"

"I want you to describe to me how you feel when you're in love, so I'll recognize it when it hits me."

She thought for a moment, then said, "You like the way a person smells and tastes—and you feel lonely and unsettled unless you're with that person. You feel that you're more *with* that person than without him."

"Did you have all of those things with Daddy?" I asked.

"Yes," she said. "You know, when we got married men used to wear starched white shirts, and taking Daddy's shirts to the laundry was one of my few extravagances because I was such a bad ironer. And in those days he smoked a bit, too. So when he would get dressed in the morning there was that lovely smell of starch plus a slight smell of tobacco—and those smells blended with the lovely natural smell of him, and it would make my heart ache when he'd leave in the morning. And each day I couldn't wait for him to come home. My love for him was so intense that if he came home a few minutes late, I'd panic. I'd think, 'Oh God, don't take this away from me.' You know, Jen, I was nice-looking but no great beauty, and I thought that if I lost Daddy, I would never be loved again.

"And when he'd come home I couldn't wait to find out everything he'd done all day and to share what I'd done. And then to share the wonder of you.

"And if we were at a party, I'd stand next to him. I'd never mingle much with the other guests. I just felt warm and sheltered and relaxed next to Daddy's great height, and I wanted all the world to see that he and I belonged to each other."

"Oh, Mom," I said, really touched by her memories, "It's all so sad. You don't know when love will strike you, and you don't know when you will lose it, and you can't do anything about it either way. It's not fair."

She wiped her eyes. "So who says anything is fair?"

"Don't tell me that. It's got to be fair. Otherwise,

nothing has any meaning. It's all so passive. According to your theory, you could even be an amoeba, a blob doing nothing, and somebody might love you. And you could be a beautiful movie actress, and nobody might. Then, even if you get love, you have no certainty of keeping it. Honestly, it's all so terrible, it's enough to make me give up."

"Look at it another way, Jen. It's so wonderful that you can always keep hoping."

"It's a terrible mystery."

"No," she laughed gently, "it's a wonderful mystery. Don't ever give up. I'm still hoping, even at my age, and you have a long life of loving ahead. You're just at the beginning of your life."

Well, I can't say I felt better after our talk, but I certainly didn't feel worse about love. As a matter of fact, it kind of did leave me hoping. *Serendipity,* my mother called it. That means something good waiting for you just around the bend, just when you least expect to find it.

In June, my cousin in New Jersey was having a graduation party. I couldn't go because I had a party of my own to attend that night, but my mother decided to go and to take Henrik along for company.

It would be the first time she had been to a family gathering since my father's defection. The party was a big fancy deal with cocktails and a sit-down lunch. I think my mother felt she could be proud of having Henrik with her, since he would definitely be one of the best-looking men around.

She probably could have taken Percy. Most of my relatives were very impressed with someone who was a college professor, even if he had gotten his doctorate in doddlelysquat. And Percy probably would have gone with her. He never could resist a free meal and a chance to impress the peasants with his erudition. But another big advantage in taking Henrik was that they could drive in his car. Our car was increasingly feeble, and my mother was afraid to take it on the parkways to New Jersey.

I sat with her while she dressed. Even though I loved her, I had to admit that she was getting a bit seedy-looking. It was a long time since she'd had money to spend on clothes; even when my father was home, she hadn't bought much. Sometimes, in the doctor's office, I'd see a copy of *Vogue,* so I knew that my mother's hemline was too short, her shoes were out of style, and her white wool sweater jacket was beginning to turn yellow. I felt kind of bad for her. She might have looked all right for an underpaid college teacher, but she didn't look right for a fancy party.

"Do you think I look all right?" she asked.

"Oh sure," I said, trying to sound convincing.

"Well . . ." She was dubious. "Maybe I'll get by."

Then Henrik arrived. He came into our living room and stood there uncertainly. He was holding a flower box and he looked terrible. I had never seen him out of uniform before. He looked great in his uniform. But now, standing there, he looked raw-boned, too big. The top of his shirt collar was frayed; his suit was shiny and old-fashioned, and besides, it was too tight for him.

He put down the flower box and asked me for a paper bag so he could empty some of the garbage out of his car. I walked to his car with him. My mother would have a fit when she saw that old heap. She had always seen him driving an official car.

This car was a ten-year-old Ford Galaxie. The paint had faded and rust spots showed through on the outside, giving a kind of rust-and-paint polka-dot appearance. The inside of the car was like a humidor; cigar ashes were over everything. The floor was littered with candy and food wrappers. One seat was torn and the stuffing showed through.

We started to empty out the junk. We couldn't do a very good job in that short a time. You would have needed a typhoon for that. We made what improvements we could, then went back inside. My mother was standing there waiting, nervous, looking as bad as he did. In fact, they were equally tacky. It made me feel very sad. I wished I could tell my mother to put on a pair of jeans and tell Henrik to go and get his uniform.

His eyes lit up. "You look absolutely beautiful," he said, handing her the flower box.

My gosh he actually meant it. I breathed a sigh of relief. She looked at the flower box curiously, without opening it.

"It's an orchid," he said proudly.

"An orchid," she responded in a horrified tone. I knew that she was really horrified about his appearance but didn't have the courage to let that show. "Why on earth did you spend money on this?" The word "this" was uttered with dismay.

His big hands fumbled. "I thought you'd like to wear it."

"This isn't a high school prom." She was close to tears. "Things have changed since high school."

"I haven't been to any parties since high school," he said sheepishly. "I just wanted to please you. You don't have to wear it."

"I wish we could give it back to the florist," she said. "It's a terrible waste of money."

"Don't worry about the money," he said. "Jen, I'd like to give it to you."

"Oh, boy!" I squealed, opening the box. "It's really beautiful. Thanks so much, Henrik. This is the second time in my life I've received flowers. The first ones were in Florida, and I got them for throwing up."

"Well," he said, "you get this flower for being Jen."

He was so nice. He made me want to cry.

"Are you ready to go?" he asked my mother.

"No, I'm a little nervous. Let's have a drink before we go. I'll make them. I have a bit of gin. Will you talk to Henrik, Jen?"

Gee, why was she getting so formal? I had talked to him many times before.

"I'd love to have a drink," he said. He was looking at her curiously, a puzzled expression on his face. He had never seen this side of her before. It wasn't a nice side and I wished I could tell him that it was because she didn't like the way she looked and she hated the way he looked.

She brought the drinks. That nice, peaceful feeling that used to exist between them was gone. I could feel the tension. They sat there, sipping their drinks, not saying anything. He tried to make conversation with me.

I guess we had both come to see Henrik as a kind of superman, but even Clark Kent doesn't look very special in his street clothes. And I suddenly realized that Henrik's speech wasn't very good, that he sounded different from the people who would be at the party.

I also realized that even his love of classical music didn't quite give him the polish of . . . well . . . I hate to use this word but it's the only way I can express what I mean. It didn't quite give him the polish of a "gentleman." My mother had made a mistake in inviting him to a party with her relatives.

Henrik finished his cigar but she made no move to get up. Finally he asked:

"What's eating you?"

"Oh nothing, nothing," she said trying to speak airily, like some kind of gay sophisticate. "I was just wondering if you'd do me a little favor at the party."

"You know I'd do anything for you, Althea," he said. "What is it?"

She hesitated for a moment then blurted out,

(four)

"When I introduce you to people at the party would you mind not telling them that you're on the Security Force? Just tell them you're an administrator here."

"I'm not an administrator," he said in a cold, tough voice, probably the voice he used on criminals, "I'm on the Security Force."

"Well," she said nervously, unable to look directly at him, "if you don't want to say that, don't say anything at all. Just don't tell them what you do."

He stood up quietly, put his drink down on the scarred coffee table, walked to the door, and out to the driveway. We heard his car start as he drove it away.

Oh mother, mother, I mourned to myself. How could you? He's such a good guy and you hurt his feelings.

My mother sat there for a few minutes. Then she went to the telephone and informed her cousin that the car had broken down and she would be unable to attend the party. She went into her bedroom, put on her nightgown, and got into bed.

I didn't know what to say or do. I took the orchid out of its box and pinned it to my hair. I liked the way I looked. I moped around for a while, listening for sounds from the bedroom, then I finally went in to see her. The TV was on and she was watching it with a strained expression on her face. I sat down beside her on the bed.

"Don't I looked pretty?" I asked her.

She looked so sad. I put my arms around her to hug her and she burst into noisy sobs. We sat like that for a few minutes, my mother sobbing, me patting her back and feeling bad about the whole thing.

When she stopped crying she said, "I have to apologize. I can't end this day without apologizing."

"Call me when you're through phoning," I said, and left her.

Fifteen minutes later, she called me. She was smiling.

"What did he say?" I asked.

"He's such a good man. He said the truth of the matter was that neither of us really wanted to go to that party. He said he hoped I'd forgive him for the orchid, but he wasn't used to a social life anymore."

"That's all?" I asked, amazed.

"That's all!"

"He wasn't angry about anything?"

"Not a bit. He said he was only sorry that I was upset."

"Wow," I said. "That's pretty nice."

(four)

"It certainly is," she agreed. "He's coming for dinner tomorrow night."

We prepared a festive dinner, but things really weren't as easy as they had been before. My mother and Henrik were both acting very polite, as if they were afraid of saying or doing the wrong thing.

After dinner, Henrik told us about a man who had invaded one of the girls' dormitories and pulled a knife on Henrik when he went to eject him.

"Scum," Henrik said. "Part of a motorcycle gang. They're all tattooed scum."

The guy had been harassing an old girl friend who lived in the dorm. When he wouldn't go away she called Security, and Henrik arrested him. But the local judge had merely fined him fifty dollars and let him go, on the condition that he leave town.

"The guy was a real psycho," Henrik said. "When we got back to the campus to get his motorcycle, he gave me the finger, then made a mad dash across the road for his bike. He raced right out into traffic. I heard the squeal of brakes and ran out, hoping I'd find his dead body."

"You don't really mean that," my mother said, aghast.

"Of course I mean it. I want him killed before he

kills somebody else. This guy's psycho, hopeless, no good to society or to himself. It he's not put away soon, he's going to hurt a lot of people."

"But that's an impossible reactionary attitude," my mother said. "Why, you probably believe in the reinstitution of the death penalty."

"You bet your life I do," Henrik countered. "You would, too, if you were on the firing line."

"There isn't anyone who can't be redeemed," my mother said angrily.

"Then how come so many of them return to jail?" Henrik asked.

"That's society's fault."

"Sometimes it is," he agreed. "But a lot of people are no damned good and they have to be done away with. Suppose it had been Hitler. Would you have refrained from killing Hitler because his problems were originally society's fault? There are people who have to be controlled for the good of society. Suppose it was Jen here that this guy had been harassing. You'd feel a lot different about it. No, I say, 'Off with their heads,' if they're a menace to society."

"Your attitude appalls me," my mother said.

"Your innocence appalls me," he said. "It's easy enough for you to talk. Other people are doing the dirty work for people like you."

(four)

I could see that this was a subject they would have to avoid in the future. I didn't really care what Henrik said. I knew he was kind and decent and noble, and he had good manners that came from his heart. I knew he'd never willingly hurt anybody.

Percy used to discuss these same things with my mother. His ideas were almost the same as hers— open the prisons, free the prisoners, legalize drugs, and blame society. Everyone would be more perfect in a more perfect society.

But Henrik thought that most people had a streak of evil in them and that it was society's duty to restrain this streak through laws. And, after all, my mother and Percy really didn't do much for society, except criticize and click their tongues in dismay. Henrik spent time every day helping people. Once you knew him, you could never again think of cops as "pigs." Whenever I thought about that expression, I got upset at the thought that it could be used toward a man like Henrik.

Henrik was having dinner with us again the following week. But he had to leave suddenly when he received a call. The same motorcyclist was back in the girls' dorm, waving his knife around. With a weary smile, Henrik said "So long" to my mother, gave me a hug, and drove off. That was the last time we ever saw him alive. We found out exactly what had happened later, from another security officer.

Henrik met this other security officer at the dorm and together they walked inside. The motorcyclist was brandishing his knife, pounding on the door of his old girl friend's room, and screaming, "Come out, bitch. Come out here. You and I are gonna have this out!"

Henrik walked up to him. "The judge ordered you not to come back here," Henrik said. "Let's go."

Before Henrik knew what was happening, the intruder rushed at him and stabbed him. He was dead in seconds.

We didn't learn about it that night, but it was all over campus the next day. My mother called Security and got the terrible details. I think it was the worst thing that had ever happened to us. Worse even than my father's defection.

We drove to the memorial service in Kingston. A huge crowd had gathered. We weren't Henrik's only friends. Lots of people got up to speak about him. One professor said that Henrik had tried to make a difference, to make the world a better place. A black man spoke and said that Henrik had worked with his parole officer to save him from going back to jail. Everyone who spoke mentioned how decent Henrik was, how selfless and kind.

My mother wept silently throughout. I had never seen her so upset. That awful feeling continued for both of us on the ride home.

"I can't go home," my mother said. "I feel a need to be where there are people. Let's get something to eat."

We rarely ate out because we couldn't afford it, but this time I agreed with her. We went to the Loaf and Tankard, our local pub. My mother ordered a double whiskey sour, and we both sat there, not able to talk. We couldn't eat what we had ordered, so we left and went home. My mother shivered when we entered the house. "I can't believe he's dead," she said.

"Me neither."

"Jen," she said, "I've been thinking all day about that terrible thing I did."

I knew she was referring to the night of the party. "He didn't stay angry," I said.

"I know. That's not what I've been thinking about. He didn't stay angry, but that doesn't change what I did. I made him feel small and insignificant.

He was better to me than almost anyone else in my entire life and I treated him worse than I've treated anyone else. He was good to me and I wanted to hurt him.

"I was ashamed of him and I was angry because I was ashamed of him. And I was angry because of what Daddy had done, and I took it out on Henrik.

"He was so kind. I looked as bad as he did, but he told me I looked lovely. He had so little money, yet he bought me that orchid. He tried so hard to please me, and I treated him so badly. I don't think I can ever forgive myself. Maybe you forgave me and he forgave me but I don't think I'll ever forgive myself. I met a fine and decent man, and I ignored the essence of the man and focused on superficialities. I will never forgive myself."

"Please don't cry, Mom," I said. I really hate to see grown-ups cry. "You were mean that one time, but you were nice lots of times. Honest, you were a good friend to him. You gave a lot to him. I think he liked knowing us to visit."

"It's not just that," she continued. "He wanted me to love him, and I couldn't love him. I wanted to, but I just didn't."

"But, Mom, that's not your fault. Didn't you tell

me that you can't make yourself love somebody? I think you were as good a friend to him as you could be."

"I feel so alone," she mourned.

"You're not alone, Mom. Remember? You have me."

She smiled and lightly stroked my face. "Yes, my darling," she said, "I have you. Thank you, God."

(*five*)

My mother

was so depressed by Henrik's death that my grand-mother decided to send her on a vacation. They picked a hotel in the Catskill Mountains. For two weeks every summer this hotel, the Stafford, caters to a singles crowd. Three thousand people converge on the hotel from every part of the United States and Canada. My mother was to spend a weekend there.

I begged to go along. Perhaps my mother and I could both find romance at the Stafford. I finally got the bright idea that a weekend at the Stafford could substitute for a sweet-sixteen party for me. On this

(*five*)

note my mother agreed—with some reluctance.

But once she had agreed, I think she was glad to have me along. She is somewhat reticent around strangers, and having me along would help her to talk to people without worrying whether she seemed aggressive or, worse yet, desperate. Like, some of my friends' divorced parents belonged to Parents Without Partners, but my mother wouldn't even fill out their application form.

"I can't see myself joining with other losers," she said.

"Why losers?" I asked.

"They all have broken marriages," she answered.

"Mom, you're not a loser," I told her. "I wish you wouldn't say things like that. I think of you as a winner."

She had smiled at that. That was when she told me she just wouldn't know how to compete for a man at any function where there were more women than men. And that was how I knew she was secretly pleased that I would be with her at the hotel.

I was kind of excited as we drove there, over the mountains, but my mother did not seem happy at all.

"It's degrading," she mumbled as she drove. "Three thousand people looking for mates. It's like some kind of primitive mating ritual. It's degrading to be a supplicant."

"I don't think it's degrading, Mom. It's just people trying to meet other people. It sounds like a good way to me, like prospecting for gold or oil or uranium. We never meet anyone sitting around the house. Maybe I'll find my Prince Charming there."

"Prince Charming in the Catskill Mountains?" She laughed.

"Sure," I said. "Why not? It's serendipity, just the way you described it."

Finally, we were there. We drove through high iron gates and had to stop at the guardhouse to give our names. The guard checked his list, then waved us in. It made me feel important. From the outside, the hotel looked like three connected apartment houses. You wouldn't believe the size of it. Can you imagine a hotel big enough to house and feed three thousand people at the same time?

All around us, boys were waving, pointing, hopping around. Everyone was whirling like a windup doll. One boy showed us where to park, another opened the car door, and a third dashed up with a cart for our luggage.

I opened the trunk and bent over to get my suitcase. I felt a pinch, let out a yelp, turned around, and saw that it was the boy with the luggage cart. I couldn't believe it.

"You pinched me," I squealed.

"That's some cute little ass," he said, "but it's not supposed to be doing my work. Trying to save on a tip? Listen, I'm not in this racket for my health. Out of my way. Loading up. Do you belong to the union? You do not. Then stay the hell away from my luggage."

All the while he was muttering he was unpacking the car trunk and piling our things neatly on a metal cart. The muttering continued: "First time here? Do you swing? What are you doing before dinner? after dinner? during dinner? Are you going to the show? Do you dig me? I dig you. Let me warn you, baby, I don't play for keeps, but I do play. Want to meet me tonight? If not, it's your hard luck, baby. There are lots of dames who really dig me. I don't have to beg from people who think they're too good for me."

During this ridiculous tirade I had said not one word. The funniest thing was he wasn't even looking at me or speaking to me. He was running through his litany like a talking machine, a makeout robot. I got the feeling that he came on that way to every guest, but he carefully avoided looking at the person to whom he was speaking, so they couldn't take him up on his offers.

I turned to face him and tried to catch his eye. "Hey," I said. "My name is Jennifer. What's yours?"

He looked at me, shocked. I had apparently violated the game rules. "Slow down, slow down," he muttered, looking nervously around him. "Want to get me fired? Boy, you sure come on strong."

Me strong? The nerve of the guy. Who had pinched whom?

The little creep loaded our luggage on the rack, stuck out his palm, and waited. "Someone else will take you to your room," he said.

My mother gave him fifty cents.

"Hey, lady," he said, "you must be kidding. Our standard rate is a dollar a suitcase. But in your case, because of the cute chick, I'll make it a dollar total."

I knew he was lying, but my mother dutifully gave him another fifty cents.

As the second bellhop approached to take our luggage, the little creep sidled up to me and muttered out of the corner of his mouth, in imitation of a gangster in an old movie, "Get rid of her and we'll really swing. I'm free from seven to seven-fifteen.

What do you say? Fifteen minutes of paradise."

"Pervert," I snapped. I dashed after my mother and the second bellhop. The place was so huge I was afraid of getting lost.

I kept feeling like Little Red Riding Hood. We got into an elevator crowded with four men in their thirties. They leered at me and licked their chops. They looked almost as if they were wearing uniforms. Each one had a big medallion hanging around his neck, a navy blue shirt open to the waist with macho hair peeping through, and a pair of tight trousers. They looked like descendants of Rudolph Valentino, only with shag haircuts, blown dry rather than slicked back. And they were equally ludicrous. They circled me.

"Hello beautiful, when did you get here?"

"Room two-eleven. We have a bar."

"Like to dance?"

"What's your dining-room assignment?"

"Can I buy you a drink?"

It was very similar to the bellhop's routine. They talked in clichés, to minimize the possibility of getting to know you. My mother might as well have been a piece of furniture. I suppose they thought I was eighteen simply because I was there.

"I'm Carlo."

"I'm Freddy."

"I'm Mario."

"I'm Tony."

"My beach chair is number thirty-seven. Meet me there and I'll smooth suntan lotion all over you."

"Didn't I see you at Roseland?"

One of them started to sing, "I Can't Get No Satisfaction," and to jit around the elevator. At last, our floor.

"Remember, you belong to me. I seen you first," one called after me as we got off the elevator.

I had said not one word to evoke such passion.

We reached our room. My mother automatically gave the bellhop a dollar, looked into the mirror, and groaned. She really felt bad about being ignored by those creeps. She called and made a beauty parlor appointment, and I decided to go to the pool.

"No suntan lotion from nobody," she joked, tousling my hair, "and no candy from strangers."

"Honestly, Mom. You must think I'm pretty stupid."

She went down to the beauty parlor and I looked at myself in the mirror. I was pretty, and I looked fresh and smooth. I hoped the beauty parlor would rejuvenate my mother. She was beginning to look dry, gray, dusty. I think as you get older you have to try a little harder. My mother was beautiful enough to me—no kid really looks at her mother critically —but I could see that she would have to shape up for the outside world. The commercials on TV and the ads in the magazines made it seem like a crime not to be pretty.

I put on the bathing suit and beach robe from our Florida trip and went down to the pool. Three young men came over to my chair as soon as I sat down. They offered me cigarettes. Everybody smoked. They smoked even more than they drank, and they drank a lot. One of the guys offered to buy me a drink. I pointed to one of the long ones. It was made of rum and fruit juice and was absolutely delicious. I felt like a movie queen with men clustered at my feet plying me with liquor and cigarettes. I wanted to giggle.

Then they started to tell me about themselves. Would you believe it, all three of them were students at Harvard Medical School? And they weren't the only ones. Later that night, every man I met was either from Yale or Harvard. I was impressed.

The three I met at the pool were rooming together.

"Want to come up to my room?" the most aggressive one asked me. "They'll stay out until we get back."

I giggled. "I'm only sixteen."

"Sixteen!"

I was left with my drink, six cigarettes, and my book. I opened *Zen and the Art of Motorcycle Maintenance* and spent the next hour happily.

When I got back to my room, my mother was already there. They had streaked her hair, cut it, and flipped it back in a short version of Farrah Fawcett-Majors' style. And she had on makeup and false eyelashes. She looked great. We put on long dresses and went down to dinner.

We were seated at a table with six other people. Four of them were from Toronto and worked together in a car-rental business. Two were men, one about forty and the other about thirty. The younger one told us that he had worked at the Stafford as a busboy when he was in college and that all his life he had dreamed of coming back as a guest. He seemed pretty normal.

The older man lived with his mother in Toronto, chomped impatiently on his cigar, and was anxious to get out to the Monticello racetrack. He ate more sour pickles and sour tomatoes than the rest of us put together and kept saying as he stuffed, "Give me a call if you ever need a car in Toronto." He gave my mother his card, which she politely put in her wallet.

The two women from Toronto worked as secretaries in the car-rental agency and were really pitiful. Even though they were still in their late twenties, they looked as if they had given up, but were still pretending to try.

Both were short and plump and had teased hair that stood out around their heads like lacquered halos. Their blouses were unbuttoned to show cleavage and their fingers were covered with fake rings. They wore toreador pants and high wedge shoes to make them look taller and slimmer, but anyone could see that they were short and plump, with stubby legs. They were just made wrong. There was nothing they could do about it except to develop nice personalities.

But their personalities were unfortunate also. They kept exchanging stage whispers about how many fellows at the hotel kept pursuing them, but I didn't believe them. And they would call out to men who were passing our table: "What's cooking,

Solly?" "Whatcha doing later, Manny?" "You're a naughty boy, Sam." Nobody answered their calls. I began to feel very embarrassed.

Of the other two people at our table, one was a woman of about sixty with a splendid figure and discontented lines around her mouth. She had beautiful hair, eyelashes an inch long, magnificent jewelry (even I could see the difference between her jewelry and that of the two Toronto women), and she smoked endlessly. She ate almost nothing, in contrast to the way the rest of us at the table pigged out.

This woman's name was Marianne. She had a great voice—husky, with a slight foreign accent. I adore exotic voices like that. She and the group from Toronto had been eating together for a week before we arrived, and it was evident that they hadn't much to say to one another. She smiled at me in a friendly way.

"You are a very pretty girl," she said.

"I think you're pretty, too," I answered. "I've never seen anyone with such gorgeous hair."

"Well," she whispered, leaning toward me, "it's a wig."

"Really? Nobody would ever know. It's gorgeous. Why do you wear it?"

(*five*)

"I am trying to look the way I used to look," she whispered.

I was fascinated. She spoke to me as if I were an adult, with seriousness.

"Why are you here?" she asked.

"I came with my mother," I said.

"I know just the boy to introduce to you tonight," she said.

"Why are you here?" I asked. "Someone as gorgeous as you should meet lots of people."

"I used to," she said. "I was married four times. But in this country, once you pass forty, you might as well be dead."

The two Toronto girls heard her and snickered. "Vunce you pass forty," they mocked her, "how about vunce you pass sixty?"

She fixed them with a contemptuous stare. "You both eat too much," she said.

I liked her a lot better than I liked them. I think it's terrible to make fun of people because they're young or old. After all, you can't help how old you are.

"At least we wear our own hair," one of the girls answered.

"Good for you," Marianne said. "I, too, have always believed in that. All animals should wear their own hair.''

She winked at me. She was really pretty cool. I enjoyed her.

The last member of our table was a hunched-over little man, not more than five feet tall, and he had a high-pitched little voice. He ate steadily, continuously, but he was annoyed by the endless whispering and giggling from the two Toronto girls. He seemed uncomfortable, too, at the possibility of an altercation between the girls and Marianne.

''Please,'' he said, shoveling in the food, ''no fighting. It's bad for my heart. My mother said I shouldn't come.''

''Ah, poor baby,'' one of the girls crooned to him. ''Want to come up to our room with us after dessert?''

He hunched farther down into his food and ignored them. What a retardate! Can you imagine asking your mother about going to a hotel when you're fifty years old?

To give you some idea of the Stafford, I want to tell you what that little man ate—grapefruit, chicken soup with dumplings, cole slaw, red cabbage salad, chopped liver, gefilte fish, roast chicken, roast beef, a side of Chinese vegetables, and then an assortment of desserts. He asked for saccharine for his tea.

My mother was close to tears. She was probably thinking about what a waste of her time and my grandmother's money it was for her to be sitting with these people. But I liked it just fine because I had never met such people before.

After dinner, the two Toronto girls asked me if I would like to play Monopoly with them. I was delighted. It was fun playing with them. When they stopped trying to act like Mae West, they were like somebody's ugly big sisters.

After the game, we went over to the Night Owl Lounge, a long room that is almost pitch dark and you keep stumbling over people's feet. Everybody seemed to think this was great fun and once, one of the Toronto girls tripped and landed in a man's lap with a thud. He took one look at her and pushed her off.

The lounge bar ran the length of the room, and people were standing along every inch of it. There were also tables to sit at and a good band for dancing in a tiny area in the center of the room. I found my mother sitting alone at a small table and sat down facing her. I ordered a Coke. It was so dark and noisy that being there was kind of dreamlike. A man came over and asked me to dance, and my mother motioned to me to go ahead and enjoy myself.

I danced with one partner after another and was having a great time. I like to dance, and here it was too noisy to hear anything but the music, so there was no need to make conversation. My mother looked bored and unhappy, but there didn't seem to be anything *I* could do for her.

Finally, the voracious little man from our table asked her to dance. My poor mother. She would never have the courage to be impolite. She stood up and towered over him, even though she was not so tall herself. I knew she wouldn't want to dance with him but after Henrik I don't think she'd ever hurt anybody's feelings again.

To my amazement, this little man was almost beautiful when he started to dance. His hunched-up body turned into a ball of graceful light on the dance floor. My mother was a rusty dancer, but he made her look good. He knew all the latest dances and was able to lead her and teach her at the same time. They danced for a half hour, then he returned her to her table and made a courtly little bow.

(*five*)

"Wasn't that amazing?" she asked me. "I had a wonderful time. I have to stop looking at every man as a potential husband and just try to enjoy people for what they are. I wish I'd understood that with Henrik."

"Please, Mom, let's not think about Henrik. Let's have a good time." And we did.

When I got back from dancing the next time, my mother was sitting talking with a man. He was pretty old, at least forty-five, and he was a lawyer. His name was Hank. Like many of the men there, he wore his shirt open to the waist, and assorted jewelry hung around his neck. I had never seen adults dress that way before. It certainly looked funny to me.

Hank smoked and drank continuously, like a kind of eating, sucking machine. My mother never drank much and couldn't keep pace with him. But she had had six whiskey sours and was getting silly and romantic, the way people do when they've had too much to drink. Occasionally Hank would take the cigarette out of his mouth, blow a puff of smoke toward her, peer into her face with his bloodshot eyes, wrinkle his nose, and say in the soppiest voice you can imagine, "Hello there, Althea Gruen."

This nonsense seemed to delight my mother, who

went off into gales of laughter every time he said it. How dumb! Believe it or not, that was the only complete sentence I heard him say until he started to complain about his wife. It seems she got fat and refused to join Weight Watchers. He couldn't stand compulsives, he said, as he chain-smoked and guzzled drinks. If a woman didn't weigh less than he did, he didn't want her.

"She just got too fat," he said.

"Too fat for what?" I asked.

"Smart kid, eh?" He leered.

I didn't understand the leer.

Hank came to the Stafford every single weekend of the year.

"Why not?" he said. "I can afford it."

And what did he do there? Did he play tennis, ice skate, swim, ski? No. Weekend after weekend he stood at the bar, waiting.

"Waiting to meet a broad I can like, like you," he told my mother. "A nice broad."

My mother winced. I knew she hated that word. I wondered where the expression came from. If a broad joke means a vulgar joke, maybe "a broad" means a vulgar woman. Just thinking about it that way made me shudder too.

It was time for the big nightclub show, in the Commodore Room, but Hank didn't want to go.

"I make a point of never going to the shows here," he said.

"But Mom," I said, "they have Anthony Hughes and I love his music. He writes and sings his own songs."

"A bum," Hank said.

"A bum?" I asked.

"Yes, yes, a bum." Hank was impatient to get rid of me, I could tell."

"Oh yeah?" I said annoyed. "What makes him a bum? Can you write or sing songs?"

"Listen," he said, "you and your mother can do what you like, but I'm not leaving this spot at the bar. I don't want anyone else to take it."

I couldn't believe it. Here was this grown-up acting like a kid about a place at a bar. Frankly, I don't think that was his real reason. I think he was too polluted at that point even to walk.

I looked at my mother. I knew she would like to go to the show—she'd been in nightclubs only once or twice in her life—but she was also flattered by the attention of this awful man. Why did she have such terrible taste in men? This one was a cross between

Percy and Sam, and she was terribly impressed because he was a lawyer. But what good is an alcoholic lawyer with a good case of lung cancer in his future? Still, I didn't want to upset her.

"It's O.K., Mom," I said. "I promised to meet Marianne outside the Commodore Room. I'll go to the show with her."

I could see my mother was grateful to me for not insisting that she go with me. I coldly said good-bye to Hank and walked toward the Commodore Room, blinking at the sudden blaze of lights. I was afraid that Marianne might have forgotten, but there she was, coolly smoking a cigarette in a long holder. Standing beside her was the first really cute guy I'd seen there. He had black curly hair, was about five feet ten and very slim.

"I was looking for you," Marianne said. "Here is the nice friend I promised you. This is Peter, the karate instructor, the nicest boy in this entire hotel, never too busy to say hello to me. Jen, meet Peter. Peter, meet Jen."

We smiled at each other.

"Now," Marianne continued, "I have reserved a good table and would like to invite you both to be my guests for the evening."

(*five*)

Peter looked at me. I looked at him. That was it. Just the way my mother had described. Everything was so nice and natural. I guess that's the way it is when things are right. Peter gave each one of us an arm. I giggled, Marianne took it gravely, and he led us into the nightclub.

Marianne counted out five dollars for the maitre d', and before you know it, we were whisked to a good table up near the platform.

The waitress came to take our drink order. Peter ordered some orange juice and I ordered a Tab.

"Peter doesn't drink or smoke," Marianne said. "He's a good boy."

"I'm the karate instructor here," Peter said. "I have great respect for my body and I'm careful about what I put into it. I also don't drink coffee or eat junk foods."

Peter was only eighteen, but he was the first sober, mature person I'd met at the hotel, excluding Marianne. He lived across the river from me, in Poughkeepsie, and his father was on the faculty of Vassar College. Peter had graduated from high school the previous June but was deferring college entrance for a year. He wanted to make some money for college. Also, he felt he couldn't go to any more classes for a while.

"All that sitting is bad for the body," he said. "I would sit there and feel my muscles deteriorating. Even the astronauts have to do exercises to keep their muscles from atrophying. But schools don't understand this. They educate the mind but do a poor job of educating the body. For example, look at the junk foods you can buy in school vending machines. Or the food they serve in lunchrooms. Carbohydrates and sweets. People can laugh if they want, but I'd eat vanilla yogurt and wheat germ for lunch instead of a bun with barbecued beef smothered in ketchup."

I was fascinated. I ate a lot of junk food. I never thought about it much before. In our town, for example, we had three fast-food places, and I always liked their tacos, hamburgers, and malts.

"How did you get interested in karate?" I asked him.

"I was mugged when I was in sixth grade," he said. "A gang of kids beat me up and took my money. I decided this would never happen to me again. So I started to attend karate classes. And while I was studying, I found out that karate is much more than a martial art—it's a philosophy, a way of looking at life."

"You mean the way the hero in "Kung Fu" is so gentle and thoughtful and compassionate?"

"Exactly," he said.

Before the evening show went on, people could dance on the stage. Peter asked me if I would like to dance.

"I'm a little embarrassed about dancing in front of an audience," I said. For those who weren't dancing were watching the dancers as if they were part of the show.

"Just think of the audience as friends who want you to have a good time," he said. "Then you won't be embarrassed."

And he was right.

Peter was a good dancer and I enjoyed being with him. He was a calm person even when he danced. No showing off. No pressing, touching, or trying to make conversation. I liked his dignity and sense of himself. He was a startling contrast with some of the grown-ups on the stage who kept nuzzling their partner's necks, performing fancy steps that looked ridiculous, perspiring and pounding. I felt very lucky being with him.

When Peter and I finished dancing, he asked Marianne to dance. She accepted graciously. She was a nice woman. She and Peter danced well together,

Peter leading her around the stage beautifully. They seemed to be having a fine time.

While we watched the show, Peter held my hand. Nothing secretive about it. Right there, on the table, where anyone could see it. He held my hand as if to say, "We'll enjoy the show more this way."

At the end of the evening Marianne took us to the coffee shop for bagels, cream cheese, and lox. Peter broke down and had an ice-cream soda.

At the door to my room he gave me a hug, just the way a good friend would. "May I come and see you next Friday night?" he asked. He worked at the hotel only on weekends.

"I'd love it," I said, not caring at all about being cool. "We'll cook a special, healthy dinner for you."

"No meat, please."

"No meat? Then what will you eat?"

"Fish, chicken, soyburgers. I'm not a vegetarian but I don't think red meat is healthy."

"We'll have just what you like," I said.

My mother was waiting for me. She was lying in bed watching TV.

"How come you're back so early?" I asked.

"I'll tell you later," she said. "First tell me what you did."

She was really happy that I'd met a nice boy and

that he was coming for dinner the following Friday. But when I asked her to tell me about her evening, she was reluctant to do so. Then she said, "I have to tell somebody."

"After you left us to go to the show," she said, slightly embarrassed, "Hank wanted to come up here with me. I said, 'I thought you didn't want to lose your spot at the bar,' and he said, 'That was just something I said to get rid of the kid. I could see you wanted to get rid of her, too.' I said that was absolutely not so and he abandoned that line of thought and said that anyway, now that we were rid of you, we should take advantage of the time and come up here. I told him I had no intention of inviting him here."

"So what happened?" I asked.

"He was quite drunk by that time, and he said, 'That's gratitude for you.' Then he said, 'You should be flattered. I was doing you a favor.'"

"How disgusting," I said. Then I giggled.

"What's funny?" she asked.

"He was funny," I said. "He was coarse and vulgar and I don't care if he is a lawyer. He looked ridiculous in his hippie beads. Even that little man you danced with was nicer."

"I'm about ready to give up the search," she said.

"Don't be upset, Mom. You are a pearl and he was a swine and that's all there is to it."

"I certainly have a lot of bad experiences," my mother moaned.

"Don't let it bother you, Mom. Marianne told me nobody has a good time on these weekends. Everybody is trying too hard."

But the next day we really had fun. We went swimming and ice skating and even began to enjoy our meal companions now that my mother had relaxed about the weekend.

All in all, I would sum it up by saying that for my mother, the weekend was almost a waste of money but for me, for me, well I had met Peter and my life looked a lot sunnier. I didn't think I'd have to spend all of my time now watching TV.

Peter called me on Thursday night and we talked for two hours. He wouldn't be able to get to my house until eight o'clock on Friday, but my mother and I like to eat late.

We really went all out to make the evening festive. We used my mother's best napkin rings, cloth napkins, her trosseau tablecloth, our best dishes, and even bought flowers for the table. I had selected the menu. First, fresh fruit cocktail, salad with my mother's famous blue cheese dressing made from scratch, and fish curry on wild rice surrounded with chopped hard-boiled egg, raisins, nuts, chutney, and plain yogurt. For dessert, my mother had made chocolate mousse. I couldn't help much because I was at school but she has no classes on Friday, so she had plenty of time.

I was dressed and nervous at six o'clock. So was my mother. The first boy I'd invited home to dinner was a special occasion. I was too restless to read or watch television. I kept floating around, looking for little distracting tasks to do, thinking of all the things I'd like to discuss with Peter, thinking about his slow, serious way of talking. I kept hoping he'd come early.

Eight o'clock came, then eight-fifteen, then nine o'clock. I was too stunned to say anything. I just sat and waited. By nine-thirty I had to face the truth. I had been stood up on my first date.

My mother looked at me so sorrowfully. "Can't you call his home?" she asked.

"Of course not," I said. "I'd be too embarrassed."

"Well I wouldn't be," she said, angrily gesturing

toward the table filled with all the expensive food and flowers.

But there was no answer at his home. Then we tried the hotel, but he wasn't there either.

"Do you want to eat?" my mother asked.

I shook my head.

Silently we started to put everything away.

(*six*)

At ten

o'clock the doorbell rang. Peter was standing there.

"Young man," my mother scolded, "my husband's worst fault was his continual lateness. I cannot excuse it in anyone else. Do you have any idea of the trouble and expense you put us to?"

"I'm terribly sorry, Mrs. Gruen," he said. "I was arrested."

"Arrested?" my mother and I squealed the word together.

I ran to him and put my arms around him. The table was still set, and my mother warmed up the curry while I put the mousse, fruit cocktail, and salad all out on the table together.

"I'm going to have some wine," my mother said.

"On this one occasion I'll bend my rules and have some myself," Peter said.

So my mother poured three glasses of wine and said, "Let's drink to Peter's safe arrival," which we did. Then we found out what had happened.

"Who arrested you?" my mother asked.

"The town police, as I was on my way here."

"It doesn't surprise me," my mother said. "They're always giving the students a hard time. Tell us what happened."

"I was driving down Main Street on my way here. A police car started to follow me, but since I wasn't speeding or doing anything wrong, I just ignored it and proceeded on my way. Suddenly another police car came out of a side street, blocking my progress, and sirens started to go off and red blinkers were flashing. Four policemen jumped out of their cars. Isn't that incredible? Four policemen with guns drawn. They told me to get out of the car and put up my hands."

"Outrageous," my mother clucked. I remembered a line from the movie of *Othello* I'd seen. "I loved him for the dangers he had passed." I held Peter's hand tightly.

"Then they put me up against the side of the car and started to frisk me," Peter continued. "That took about fifteen minutes. When they didn't find anything on me, they proceeded to examine the car, minutely, every inch of it, even under the carpet. I'm sure they were looking for drugs. Then they got to the glove compartment where they found my nunchucks."

"They're absolutely paranoid about drugs in this town," I muttered.

"What are nunchucks?" my mother asked.

"Two sticks connected by a leather thong," Peter answered. "I use them in my karate teaching."

"Then what happened?" I asked.

"They handcuffed me and asked why I was carrying a dangerous weapon. I explained that I use nunchucks in my teaching, but they didn't believe me. I think they were sore because they didn't find any drugs and were going to pick on anything they could find to justify the time they had wasted on me. Anyway, they put me in one police car and drove me to the courthouse."

"Were you scared?"

"Not then, but I was afterward. My hands are so flexible from karate that I was able to slip out of the handcuffs and be more comfortable. I held the handcuffs on my lap. I had never been in handcuffs before. It's a frustrating feeling. Well, one of the policemen turned around, saw the handcuffs on my knee, and let out a yelp. They stopped the car, handcuffed me again, and then one of them held a gun to my head all the way to the court."

" 'One false move out of you,' " he said, " 'and I'll blow your head off.' "

"Outrageous!" my mother said.

"I got to court and wanted to telephone you, but they said I had to wait. Finally, Judge Rexford Slyder came in."

"He's not a real judge," my mother said contemptuously. "He's the local butcher. He acts as a justice in his spare time."

"Do you mean that literally?" Peter asked.

"Literally. He actually works as a butcher."

Peter looked amazed. "The police told Judge Slyder about my case. I think he was angry, too, that they hadn't found any drugs. He yelled at me for wasting the court's time. Then, without letting me speak, he said 'Guilty' and fined me fifty dollars for carrying a concealed weapon. When I objected, he gave me a choice of paying the fine or going to jail. So I paid."

"It's like frontier justice," my mother said. "Let me get this straight. Without your saying a word, without being able to explain to him that you use the nunchucks in your work, without a trial, he found you guilty?"

Peter nodded.

"Do your parents know?" my mother asked.

"They're away."

"I wish you'd called us, Peter. I would have given that judge a few words he wouldn't forget."

"I tried to phone," he said bashfully. "I asked if I could call my girl friend, but they wouldn't let me."

His *girl friend*. I exulted inside myself. He called me his girl friend. Instead of being concerned about injustice, all that mattered to me at that moment was that at last someone had called me his girl friend.

"You sound surprisingly calm about losing the fifty dollars," my mother said.

"I'm not," Peter said gloomily. "I was so angry that if I hadn't worried about you, I would have gone to jail until my parents returned. My father will insist on hiring a lawyer and getting my money back."

How wonderful to have that kind of father, I thought.

"I hope he can," my mother said seriously, "or those fingerprints and mug shots are going to go on your record and haunt you for the rest of your life. I learned a lot about these things when I was teaching at the prison."

"Don't worry," he said. "I think my father can do something. And I'm here now, and your food is just great."

Then my mother did something really nice. She walked over to him, put her arms around him gently, and gave him a kiss on the cheek. It was as if she were welcoming him to the family.

"Well," he grinned at me, "I'm waiting."

So I ran over to him and gave him a kiss on the cheek, too.

"Thank God you're safe," my mother said. All the vibrations between the three of us were so lovely. So this is what it feels like to have a happy family, I thought.

After that I saw Peter every Friday night. We didn't do much, but we were happy. We liked to swim, so many nights we went swimming at the college. Twice he took me to karate competitions, but I didn't like the ones he was in. I saw people get hurt, and didn't want that to happen to him.

We talked on the phone every night. His folks had a really nice house in Poughkeepsie, and after we had known each other for a while, sometimes I would spend a few days there with him.

Both his parents taught, so I didn't get to see them much, but he had many friends in Poughkeepsie. One of them had a boat on the Hudson River. There always seemed to be more to do in Poughkeepsie than in New Paltz. There were four movie theaters, better discos, and a civic center with ice skating. And great concerts. Peter was a good horseback rider and he taught me to ride, too.

Summer is my favorite season. There's always so much to do. Peter showed me a waterfall, far into the mountains near Lake Minnewaska, where students from the college swung from ropes like Tarzan and even swam in the nude. I wore a bathing suit. But Peter was perfectly free and natural about being naked.

My mother was teaching summer session at the college, but I was so busy with Peter that I almost forgot about her needs. Sometimes I would stay for two or three days at Peter's house, and just call my mother to tell her where I was.

In mid-July, Peter had to go to a karate camp in

Vermont. Once more, I was thrown back to my mother for companionship. I was kind of surprised when I took a good look at her one morning. She had become very quiet and very plain. In the mornings she went to classes; in late afternoon, she returned home and prepared dinner. We ate dinner without talking much, watched TV, to which she now had become addicted, and went to bed.

The last time I remembered hearing her laugh was at our dinner for Peter, when we sat around drinking wine and liking each other. She used to talk so much. Now she was quiet and sad. She didn't ask me much about Peter, about his home, or his parents, or what we did. Conversation seemed like too much of an effort for her. If I talked, she'd appear to listen, but I could tell that what I was saying didn't really register.

I wondered how she was doing in her teaching. Maybe nobody noticed how defeated she was. She had been known for her energy and enthusiasm. Maybe she now seemed more like the other teachers.

I could feel how lonely she was. I was lonely, too, with Peter away. I didn't like this kind of life. I wanted people and parties, brothers and sisters, fighting and making up, laughing and making noise. I wanted the bustle of family life, the kind of bustle that makes me feel alive. Anything was preferable to this boredom, this maleless house, this emptiness that made me feel hollow in the pit of my stomach, as if I were hungry.

I had received a letter from my father. He would be back at the end of the summer and would return to school for the fall semester; he couldn't wait to see me. But he didn't say if he would be living with us or not. He asked me to show the letter to my mother and give her his warm regards. I guess he was afraid to write directly to her.

"Do you think Daddy will be coming back here to live?" I asked her.

"I don't know," she answered quietly.

"Would you let him?"

"I don't know. I don't care."

But while we waited, my mother was getting pretty weird. I couldn't talk to anyone about her without feeling disloyal. Also, I didn't know exactly what I could say. It wasn't that she did anything peculiar— unless you had known what she was like before. Sometimes she reminded me of Captain Ahab, in *Moby Dick,* in the part where he throws his pipe and sextant overboard, and this symbolizes his cutting himself off from civilization. That seemed to be just what my mother was doing.

Her radio had broken, and she didn't have it repaired. The TV had broken down, and that hadn't been fixed either. I watched TV on an old black-and-white set we had in the basement. My mother stayed in her bed much of the time, trying to read, studying the ceiling.

"When you go to boarding school in September," she said wearily one day, "I'll have the phone taken out. Nobody calls me. Anyway, anyone who wants to can reach me on my office phone."

Paint was chipping and wallpaper was peeling. My mother taught, collected her paycheck, made dinner, ate, and lay on her bed. Gradually I took over the shopping, cooking, and cleaning. Part of me watched what was happening to her with loving concern. But I have to admit that another part of me began to be annoyed and resentful. I wanted to be happy, to be free, to do things with Peter when he returned. I didn't want to feel guilty about how unhappy my mother was.

Peter's family had a summer house in Stowe. They invited me to spend a few weeks there with Peter. I was afraid to tell my mother and put off telling her until the day before his return. She was lying on her bed, as usual, looking at the ceiling.

"What are you thinking about?" I asked her.

"Two stories," she said. "Two things that happened and that I did nothing about. Two stories that haunt me. One of them happened long ago, when I was returning to New York from a summer session at the University of Mexico. My father didn't want me to fly, so I had a compartment on a train. Just before I got on the train, I ran into a black dental student I'd met at the university. He was going home to Baltimore, but since he would have had to sit up all the way, I invited him to ride with me during the day. We rode along singing folksongs; songs by Woody Guthrie and Pete Seeger. He had a guitar and played a song I had never heard before, "I've Got the World on a String." I loved that song. Still do, in fact. When we got to Marshall, Texas, the train stopped. Two policemen got on the train, knocked on my door, handcuffed my friend, and took him off the train for being with a white girl. I stood there weeping.

" 'What can I do?' I asked the black Pullman porter.

" 'Nothin. Just sit tight. You'll only make it worse if you interfere.'

"I stood there. His luggage was left on the train. I hope they didn't beat him or imprison him. It was awful, and I think I was cowardly. I should have gotten off the train, too. I had no way of finding out what happened to him. I never even knew his last name. One minute we were singing and the next, he was gone. And it was my invitation that got him into trouble."

"What's the other story?" I asked. I was interested, and I was also pleased that she was talking with *some* animation.

"The other story happened right here at Vassar Hospital when you were a little girl. Remember, you stubbed your toe on somebody's pool and I took you to the emergency room? While we were waiting, two men with beer bellies and flushed faces helped each other in. One sat down and the other went out to park his car. When he returned, he helped his friend up to the desk to check in. They both seemed pretty drunk to me.

"I heard them tell the woman at the desk that they had been walking along the railroad track and a chain had suddenly swung out from a train and cracked the smaller man in the head. When you looked closely, you could see that he was in pain.

"They both sat down then, the big man belching

and the little one groaning in pain. Then a cop came in.

" 'What were you doing in the railroad yard?' he asked.

" 'Go away, man,' the little one groaned, holding on to his head, 'can't you see I'm hurtin?' I can't answer any questions.'

" 'You *are* going to answer a few questions,' the officer insisted.

" 'Look, I'll be back later,' the big man said. He practically sprinted to the door, got in his car, and drove off. I guess he didn't want to get involved with the law."

"That wasn't a nice thing to do, Mom," I said.

"Oh, I agree. Anyway, the cop and the hurt man continued to have words. The cop kept saying, 'Just tell me what you were doing there,' and the little man kept saying, 'I don't have to answer no questions.'

"Finally, the cop ran out of patience. 'On your feet,' he ordered. He handcuffed the little man and dragged him out. Then they went off in the police car."

"That's terrible," I said indignantly. "Why didn't the people in the hospital say something?"

"I don't know if anyone was aware of what was

happening. The point is that *I* should have said something. I should have reminded the policeman that someone *was* watching, that the little man was in pain, might have a skull fracture. I knew he was hurt. I should have said something. Instead, I just sat there."

"Why do those stories haunt you, Mom?" I asked.

"Because I didn't like myself then, and I don't like myself now. I was passive then, and I'm passive now. I don't take action. I just let things happen."

"Well," I said, "you can't take action on anything if you spend all your free time lying in bed and looking at the ceiling."

"I know," she said gloomily.

This was the time to tell her about Stowe. "Mom," I said, "I'm invited to Peter's summer house for a couple of weeks, maybe for the rest of the summer. Please, please try to do something to save your summer. If I think you're just teaching and lying here, I'll feel too guilty to have fun.

"It's not fair. I'm sixteen. I want to feel happy and free, not worried all the time. Please, Mom, if you feel guilty about the past, do something now. You couldn't make a difference to that student or to the man in the hospital, but you can make a difference to me. Please, Mom."

She sat up and took me in her arms. "Of course, darling. You go along and have a good time, and I promise you things will be different when you return. I promise you. You don't have to worry anymore."

Peter and I had a great time in Vermont, hiking, water skiing, bicycle riding, just goofing around. Each day was especially joyous. I had never had a special friend my own age to do these things with before. There are some people who make you better than you are. That's the way I was with Peter. We were good friends.

I called home twice. My mother was fine and cheerful both times, not like a walking nervous breakdown. I listened carefully but it didn't sound as if she were only putting on an act for me.

When I went home in mid-August, everything was different. The house was clean and had been freshly painted inside and out. My mother looked great, and she was cheerful. I wondered what had brought about these changes.

Remember how my mother tried to form a women's group at the college? Well, a year had passed since then, and things were different now. There was an active women's group in the town and my mother had joined it. They met once a week, just to talk, and my mother had arranged for them to meet next at our house.

Six pretty, nice, friendly women came to the meeting. They sent out good vibrations to me. All of them had sad stories to tell, yet they all seemed cheerful and liberated. So did my mother.

One woman still seemed bitter as she said, "All of us have been kicked around all our lives by men. So, after the first experience, did we get smart? Did we give up men the way we'd give up smoking or drinking? No, we kept running back for more of what had made us unhappy in the first place. All of us were miserable with men, but we felt life would be miserable *without* them. We were never able to figure out the illogic of *that* position."

"It's like parochial school," another said. "My mother had nightmares all her life about her Catholic elementary school so what did she do when she had kids? Sent us all right back to the very school situation that had traumatized her for life."

My mother said, "In a good relationship, you have a built-in friend and companion. I think life is better with a man."

"But at what price?" another woman asked.

"That's the question," my mother said. "It's hard to know when you're paying too high a price. I mean, if we're honest, even if two women are friends, they have to bend and be flexible and adjust to each other. Parents have to do that with children, and people have to do that with the neighbor next door. The question is, how much is enough bending and adjusting and how much is too much?"

"I know when it's too much," I piped up. They had told me I could speak if I wanted to. "I think you're paying too high a price if you like yourself less because of the situation. You see, I go with this boy, Peter, and whenever we're together, I like myself more." I felt good about contributing my ideas, and the women were quick to respond.

"My husband doesn't make me feel better about myself," one woman said.

"My ex-husband didn't either," said another.

"Of course," my mother broke in, "another question is, do we make them feel better about *themselves?* I can honestly say that I don't think I did that for my husband." I liked my mother's sense of fair play.

"That's very true," someone said. "You know, men have problems too, very serious problems. They have to worry about image and potency and making a living."

"One thing I've come to understand from this group," another woman said, "is that I shouldn't limit myself for emotional support just to a husband or a boy friend. No one person can be everything. It causes too heavy a burden. We have to reach out to many people for support. I feel as if the love and friendship I've found in this group has enriched my life—practically saved it."

"What I've come to understand from this group," my mother said, "is that if I won't put up with certain behavior from a woman, I shouldn't put up with it from a man. When I remember some of the irresponsible things my husband did, I see that I would not have had a woman friend who did such things."

"Yes," another woman said, "if I wouldn't care to spend time with a certain type of woman, I'm not going to spend time with that type of person just because he's a man. I could kick myself for some of the dates I've gone on. I pretended to be interested when I would have been happier at home reading a good book."

"Right," a third woman said. "I'm not going to have lower and different standards for someone just because he is a male. In the same way, I don't want a man to have different standards about me because I'm a woman. I don't want him to be surprised when I manage a checkbook well and drive a car well. I don't want him to assume that I'm clothes crazy. In return for that, I would promise not to expect him to be strong and capable all the time."

"The thing is," my mother said, "to be able to face honestly what isn't good, and not to pretend that it is good out of fear of abandonment. We have to see that the world is full of human beings—and only some of them can help us to grow, can make us feel better about ourselves." Then she looked at me tenderly and said, "That's the kind of help I've received this past year from Jen. Nobody could have done more for me than she has."

I couldn't believe my mother said that. I felt so proud.

Each woman kissed me good-bye as she left. They certainly were fine women, and knowing them had made a fine change in my mother.

As we cleaned up the dishes, my mother said to me, "Daddy called. He'll be home tomorrow."

I felt shocked. I don't know why. He *had* written to me, but I hadn't known the exact day. My God,

I realized how much I had missed him. I started to cry.

My mother waited until I wiped my eyes. I asked, "Is he coming with his girl friend?"

"No," my mother said. "That's all over. She left him for a Danish student. Apparently she decided he was too old."

"Serves him right," I said. "Did he say anything about staying with us?"

"No, we haven't discussed anything. We'll talk tomorrow."

Oh pure joy. I couldn't stay mad at him. After all, he was my father. I had loved him for all of my life. You can't just switch those feelings off, even if someone does defect.

The next day when I came home my father was sitting at the kitchen table as if he had never left.

"Daddy!" I screamed. I ran over to him and hugged him. Then I cried a little and he wiped his eyes and I sat down, unable to hide my happiness at the sight of him.

He had a present for me. "It's a belated sweet-sixteen present," he said.

It was one of those multicolored Finnish ski sweaters. I loved it. It was the most expensive, beautiful sweater I had ever owned.

"And here's a matching one for you," he said, with that same old heartbreaking smile, as he held out a package to my mother. When she did not reach for it, he put it down on the table and pretended not to notice.

"Shall I set the table for dinner?" I asked.

"Am I invited?" he asked.

"You are certainly welcome to have dinner with us," my mother said, calmly and firmly.

So we ate and we chatted. I couldn't believe my father. He seemed to have no awareness of what we had been through.

"Althea," he said, "you would have loved Denmark."

"I guess I would have," she said.

We finished dinner. Peter was picking me up later. I wished the time would hurry by so I could escape from the two of them.

"Althea," he said, "I have to know whether or not you'll let me move back. Before the semester starts, I have to get settled and get my course outlines done."

"Just like that?" my mother asked.

He flashed her his most dazzling smile. I had to admit it. He was still the handsomest man around.

"I suppose you want me to say I'm sorry," he said. "All right, I'm sorry. Now may I move back in?"

"What about my feelings? What about me?" my mother asked.

"Oh, I know, you feel hurt and embarrassed in front of everyone. I know just what you're going to tell me. And I suppose you want to get even with me and make me crawl a bit and I'm willing to eat humble pie for a while but, after all, must you take your pound of flesh? How will making me miserable make up for this past year?"

"You're absolutely right. Nothing will make up for this past year," my mother said.

"I'll get my bags," he said.

"Did it never occur to you that I might not want you back?" she said.

He looked at her in genuine puzzlement. "Of course it didn't," he said. "This is my house," he said. "Jen is my daughter, too. I told you I'd be back. Lots of couples have separated for a time."

"Usually," my mother said, "in that kind of separation both people are parties to it."

"I knew it, I knew it," he said looking tragical, "you always were the kind of person to carry a grudge." She laughed.

"I really love you and Jen. Don't you believe that?" he asked.

"I suppose you think you do," she said. "But it's not my kind of love. Do you remember that Dr. Seuss book we used to read to Jen, *Horton Hatches the Egg*? When the Maisie bird lays her eggs and flies off to Florida, Horton, being a responsible animal, has no choice but to sit on the eggs. And he sits and he sits, through all kinds of weather and all kinds of discomfort. When the Maisie bird finally returns Horton doesn't need her anymore—and neither do the eggs. That's how I feel about you. You left me alone to maintain our nest and care for our darling daughter, and I found that I could do just fine all by myself. You made yourself superfluous."

"You'll still need money, for the house and for Jen," he said.

"I hope you'll give me some," my mother said. "But I've managed for over a year by myself. I think I can continue to manage."

"Believe me, Althea, I never loved that girl." My father sounded sincere.

"I'm sure you loved her for a time; as much as you love Jen and me. But I'm not jealous anymore.

And that has nothing to do with my decision."

"Is there another man?" he asked.

"No," my mother said. "I wish there were."

"I'm trying to understand," he said. He had the dazed look of a bull who has been injured in the ring.

"You say there's no man and you're not jealous and yet you won't have me back?"

"That's right."

"Well, we'll just see about that." He was getting angry now. "This is my house and I have every right to be here."

And then they were off. She complained about his not helping with the chores, and she complained about his worshipping students. He complained that she never praised him. She said she never had anything to praise. She complained that he was always irresponsible and he reminded her that he had always turned over every paycheck to her.

I listened with interest but without panic. They couldn't upset me anymore. I had heard all of these complaints and accusations all through the years I was growing up. They were almost predictable by now. I did feel sad that neither one of them had changed in relation to the other. Not Daddy with

(*six*)

his year in Denmark and not Mother, either, with her succession of boy friends or her women's lib group.

Finally, he asked:

"Then you really won't take me back?" He was bewildered.

"I can't," she said.

"Don't you love me anymore?"

"I'll always love you," she said, "but I can't live with you again."

The air seemed to rush out of him. He sat there looking tired, puzzled, deflated.

"Where will I go?" he asked weakly.

"Don't worry," my mother said. "If you could find an apartment in Denmark without speaking Danish, I'm certain you'll be able to manage here."

"Oh Daddy," I cried running to him. I threw my arms around him; tears were streaming down my face.

"Don't cry, Jen," he said.

"See," he said to my mother, "Jen wants me to stay."

I wiped my eyes. He hadn't understood that I was weeping for him. It was terribly hard but I had to do it.

"No Daddy," I said. "It's not that I don't want you

to stay, but I think Mom has to keep growing up by herself."

He didn't understand. He turned to her accusingly:

"I can't believe you don't have someone else," he said.

"I do have someone else," she said. "I have *me!*"

He was still bewildered.

"Well," he said, "if I have to get a motel room, I'd better get going. Are you sure I can't stay just this one night?"

She shook her head.

"What'll I do about my laundry?"

"Leave your laundry, Daddy," I said. "I'll be glad to do it—any time you like."

I walked him to the garage and kissed him good-bye.

"I love you, Daddy," I said. "Don't worry. I think everything will work out all right."

"I love you, too," he said.

I walked back into the kitchen. My mother's shoulders sagged. There were tears in her eyes.

"Was that hard, Mom?" I asked. She nodded.

"Did you really want him to stay?"

"Yes, of course, I'll always love him."

"You love him but don't want to live with him?"

"The truth is," she said, "we aren't good for each other any more. I don't know if we can grow if we are not together, but I am certain that we can't grow if we live together. I would go right back to being a warden, and he would go right back to being a rebellious prisoner."

She wiped her eyes and gave me a little smile.

"You know what, Mom? I think you're pretty sensational."

"You know what, Jen, I think I'm pretty sensational too. And so are you!"

We put our arms around each other and lovingly hugged.

I heard Peter honking the car horn in the driveway.

"Is it all right if I go out?" I asked. "I don't want you to be lonely."

"Run along now and find Peter. Don't even think about me. I won't be lonely."

I gave her a kiss. "I love you," I said.

"And I love you, my darling," she answered.

I got into the car and snuggled close to Peter's side. Then I told him my father was back but my mother wouldn't take him home.

"That's kind of sad," he said. "How do you feel about it?"

"If she were doing it to get even, I would think it was wrong," I said. "But that's not why. It's as if she started growing while he was away, and he remained the same. She's not the same person anymore."

Then I started to cry. "Oh Peter, it was really so awful. He seemed so pathetic, so vulnerable. It's sad because he doesn't seem to understand what he did. But it's better to have him go. This way, they can each find people they're better suited for."

I cried for a few more minutes while Peter patted my back and gave me warmth.

I finished crying, blew my nose, and looked up at him.

"And now?" he asked gently.

"And now," I said holding him close, "it's time for me to start worrying about myself."

SHEILA SCHWARTZ is well known in the fields of education and adolescent literature as teacher, author, consultant and reviewer. She has taught at a number of universities both here and abroad and is now Professor of English Education at the State University College in New Paltz, New York. Dr. Schwartz was born and grew up in New York City and now lives with the youngest of her three children in New Paltz. Like Mother, Like Me *is her first novel.*